Landmarks on a Trail of Blood

A hideous cage of cruelty created by a father for his son—a cage from which there is only one unspeakably grisly escape . . .

A death ship sailing through a shark-infested sea—a ship captained by a demon in human form . . .

An immensely powerful wolf tamed by man—a wolf that for the first time hears the call of violence in its blood . . .

An arctic wasteland of blinding snow and raging winds—a wasteland where the line between man and beast freezes over . . .

The spectre of ultimate evil conjured up by a mind on the brink of madness—a spectre that one day comes knocking on the door . . .

These are just five of the unforgettable confrontations with fear awaiting you in—

THIRTEEN TALES OF TERROR
By Jack London

THIRTEEN TALES OF TERROR

Published by Fawcett Popular Library, a unit of CBS Publications, the Consumer Publishing Division of CBS Inc.

Introduction copyright © 1978 by John Perry

All Rights Reserved

ISBN: 0-445-04254-0

Printed in the United States of America

9 8 7 6 5 4 3

Thirteen Tales Of Terror by Jack London

Edited and with an Introduction
by John Perry

FAWCETT POPULAR LIBRARY • NEW

Contents

Publishing History

"A Thousand Deaths." *The Black Cat*, May, 1899. Uncollected.

"The White Silence." *Overland Monthly*, February, 1899. *Son of the Wolf* (short story collection), 1900.

"In a Far Country." *Overland Monthly*, June, 1899. *Son of the Wolf*, 1900.

"Even unto Death." *San Francisco Evening Post Magazine*, July 28, 1900. Uncollected.

"The Man with the Gash." *McClure's Magazine*, September, 1900. *God of His Fathers* (short story collection), 1901.

"The One Thousand Dozen." *The National Magazine*, March, 1903. *Faith of Men* (short story collection), 1904.

"Bâtard." *The Cosmopolitan*, June, 1902. *Faith of Men*, 1904.

"The Dominant Primordial Beast," from *The Call of the Wild*. Serialized in *The Saturday Evening Post*, June 2–July 18, 1903. Novel published 1903.

"The Death of Ligoun." *Children of the Frost* (short story collection), 1902.

"In the Forests of the North." *Pearson's Magazine*, September, 1902. *Children of the Frost*, 1902.

"Keesh, the Son of Keesh." *Ainslee's Magazine*, September, 1902. *Children of the Frost*, 1902.

"The God of His Fathers." *McClure's Magazine*, May, 1901. *God of His Fathers* (short story collection), 1901.

from *The Sea Wolf*. Serialized in *The Century Magazine*, January–November, 1904. Novel published 1904.

INTRODUCTION

by John Perry

Terror!

It stalks through the stories of Jack London
from the Yukon's white wilderness to the tropi-
cal South Seas. Always the same. Death trips
man somewhere on the edge of civilization
where "the struggle for survival continued to
wage with all its ancient brutality." He freezes
on Klondike trails. Fierce wolves devour him
alive. Bloodlust brutes break his bones. Hunger
saps his spirit. Loneliness drives him insane.

Such is the weird world of Jack London,
where only the strongest of the strong survive,
where sinister shadows and crouching fears de-
ment man's mind. Here reason fails. Logic
stumbles beneath the grip of irrational forces.
Just muscle counts, whether it's Wolf Larsen in
The Sea Wolf, who jumps nine feet and pulver-
izes people with meat-hook hands, or Buck in
The Call of the Wild, "the dominant primordial
beast who had made his kill and found it good."

Trails of spattered blood. These became London's trademark. Carl Van Doren said that he
"carried the cult of red blood in literature to an
extreme at which it began to sink to the ridicu-

lous." Why such sadism? Why the soured life-view? Alfred Kazin believes that London's "thick slabs of bleeding meat were essentially only a confession of despair." Perhaps his strange childhood provides clues to such wretchedness.

London was born on 12 January 1876, the result of a brief affair between footloose astrologer William H. Chaney and spiritualist Flora Wellman. A bad start for any infant. Eight months passed. Flora married John London whom she dominated, eventually ruining him with astrological charts, Chinese lottery tickets, and get-rich-quick schemes. The millions who later read *White Fang*, *The Sea Wolf*, and *The Call of the Wild* never knew about London's bastardy. It remained his biggest shame and secret—hidden until twenty years after his death in 1916.

"A Thousand Deaths," one of London's earliest stories, shows these gnawing anxieties about William H. Chaney, a character whom the narrator calls "not a father but a scientific machine. I wonder how it ever came to pass that he married my mother or begat me, for there was not the slightest grain of emotion in his make-up." In this lurid tale, a scientist experiments on his own son, leading to a thousand deaths, some causing intense pain. The son finally seeks a bizarre revenge.

What kind of child was Jack London? A loner with few friends, a smallish fellow with weak wrists and sensitive skin who lost scraps with bigger boys, but held long-time grudges. Books nourished his fantasies. He read Ouida's *Signa*, an Italian romance about a gifted peasant boy, a biography of Garfield that proved that someone with grit could become President, and the Horatio Alger type of dime novel. All peddled the American "rags-to-riches" myth.

It wasn't long, however, before time eroded London's fact-fancy pipe dreams. The streets taught harsh lessons. So did knuckle talk. He soon called man "a monstrous spectre" and "disease of the agglutinated dust." Civilization? It was a glossy veneer that hid man's savagery:

"As for the primitive. I hark back to it because we are still very primitive," he once said. "How many thousands of years of culture, think you, have rubbed and polished at our raw edges? One probably; at the best, no more than two. And that takes us back to screaming savagery, when, gross of body and deed, we drank blood from the skulls of our enemies, and hailed as highest paradise the orgies and carnage of Valhalla."

After knocking around the San Francisco waterfront with hoodlums and wharf rats, London hit the adventure path: He sailed on a sealing schooner to the Bering Seas. He bummed across country, riding the rods of freight trains, begging handouts. He worked for slave wages in a cannery, jute mill, and steam laundry. He even attended the University of California at Berkeley for one semester. His big break? The Yukon gold rush of 1897-98.

Although London didn't find yellow dust, he stored impressions of tinhorns and sourdoughs,

traveled to Dawson several times and absorbed
the land's eerie desolation. All this he turned
into hard cash, writing dozens of Klondike stories and two dog novelettes that have sold millions—*White Fang* and *The Call of the Wild*. He
became America's highest-paid author, although he hated the writing game, preferring to
run free.

But despair clutched London's life. That's
why he called men maggots, wiggling worms,
and brute beasts. (Buck in *The Call of the Wild*
and White Fang are men hidden beneath dog
fur.) The death-wish haunted him. Yet, like the
misbegotten missionary in "The God of His Fathers," London clung to life, that elemental
urge: "But the love of life! the love of life! He
could not strip it from him."

Confused by complex neuroses, an obsession
that the strong survive—especially Anglo-Sax-
ons—and a lust for materialistic gain, London's
life separated at the seams. He grew old prema-
turely. He suffered agonizing illnesses. He
drank. His career even faltered. Existence became insufferable. Much of this, of course, is
mirrored in his novels and short stories.

London expressed his world-weariness in tales
of cruel sadism, primordial passion, and lawless
bloodlust. Even the wolf became his symbol of
savage power and endurance: He used the name
in the titles of *The Sea Wolf* and *The Son of the
Wolf*. He had a wolf's head on his stationery and
bookmarks. He signed his letters wolf. He
named a massive ranch Wolf House. Characters
wore wolf-skin caps. As Sidney Alexander re-

marked, "The trouble with Jack London was that he wasn't sure whether he was a man or wolf."

The most macabre touch? London liked raw beef sandwiches. About the *13 Tales of Terror*:

"The White Silence" sets the terrible tone of London's Klondike stories, a voiceless void that hates movement. It tries to still the blood of men who violate these ageless icescapes that threaten the will to be. "Sole speck of life journeying across the ghostly wastes of a dead world, he trembles at his audacity, realizes that his is a maggot's life, nothing more." But nature's silent menace tricks both the weak and strong, the foolish and the wise. Few escape her icy coffin. Even Mason, an experienced journeyman, is reduced to "the pitiable thing," dying in torment.

Percy Cuthfert and Carter Weatherbee, two tenderfeet who spend the winter together in a miserable ten by twelve foot cabin, also become victims of the "ghastly silence" in "In a Far Country." They hoard sugar, keep eyes glued on cocked revolvers, and hallucinate. When they don't recognize each other in a thicket, "they sprang to their feet, shrieking with terror, and dashed away on their mangled stumps; and falling at the cabin door, they clawed and scratched like demons till they discovered their mistake."

The sugar-sack dooms both men.

Frona Payne also flips in "Even Unto Death." When her brawny lover leaves for Forty Mile, he swears that "even unto death, I shall claim you, and no mortal man shall come between!" After he dies of frozen lungs, Frona forgets these prophetic remarks and finds another Klondike King. But an unpainted pine box leaves her a raving madwoman.

Jacob Kent, who rents cabin bunks to wayfarers in "The Man with the Gash," joins this deranged set. His greatest fear? Someone will steal precious sacks of hidden gold-dust, especially the man with a "gash on his right cheek" who oppresses his dreams. The inevitable happens. When this man appears at Kent's doorstep, his greed for gold provokes an ironic and frightful finish.

The curse of money madness also convulses David Rasmunsen in "The One Thousand Dozen." His fortune's folly? To make thousands from selling eggs in the frozen wastes. He suffers hell on frosted trails to Dawson: He loses two toes in a blizzard. He starves. His foot freezes "so that a running sore developed, into which he could almost shove his fist." He even pulls in the traces when several dogs die. All for eggs.

But Rasmunsen makes a fatal mistake. And that leads to disaster in a smoke-filled room on the raw edge of the world.

More tantalizing terrors? Try London's wolf-dog stories.

"Bâtard" is a devil dog whom Klondikers call "Hell's Spawn." His master Black Leclère is even worse. These two fiends despise each other. "Their hate bound them together as love could never bind." Although Leclère brutally beats the beast, he still protects him from the cold, hunger, and other animals, waiting for the right murderous moment. Bâtard also waits to sever Leclère's jugular vein. The ending? A real shocker.

Bâtard and Buck in *The Call of the Wild* represent cosmic evil. Both are cruel killers. Both are called devils. Both find the bloodlust kill "an ecstasy that marks the summit of life, and beyond which life cannot rise." London even patterned *The Call of the Wild* on "Bâtard."

Buck is kidnapped from a ranch in California's Santa Clara Valley and shipped to the freezing Yukon, where he becomes part of the primitive "dog eat dog" wasteland. He learns fast: Only the strong survive. The weak become burger. His brute strength and superior intelligence pay off. "He was ranting at the head of the pack, running the wild things down, the living meat, to kill with his own teeth and wash his muzzle to the eyes in warm blood."

The climax of "The Dominant Primordial Beast" pits Buck against Spitz, who challenges his leadership in the traces. A death struggle ensues.

Jack London also wrote blood-vengeance Indian stories. "The Death of Ligoun" is a chilling ritual of an old chieftan who prefers to die "when the blood leaps to the knife." During a lodge feast, he's defiled by a boastful brave who slashes his face. "Old hates flamed up" and the "blood-hunger" grips everyone's senses, leading to a frenzied slaughter that few survive.

Blood-vengeance also soaks "In the Forests of the North." When another old Indian allows his daughter to mate with a white man, a rival warrior threatens, "And the meat of no man's kill tastes as sweet as the meat of my kill." A quivering arrow ends this vendetta.

"Keesh, the Son of Keesh," another blood-curdler, is about a peace-loving Indian who has forsaken "the song of the bowstring in battle." But Keesh wants Su-Su, daughter of the tribe's chief, who accuses: "Since thou left the Raven to worship the Wolf, thou art become afraid of blood, and thou makest thy people afraid." Su-Su gives Keesh an ultimatum: Bring her at least three heads, all dripping with fresh blood. He fills the order. Su-Su shudders at the gory sight.

"The God of His Fathers" remains one of London's most venomous attacks on civilized ethics. Baptiste the Red, a half-breed Indian whose "hands were wet with blood," seeks vengeance against the church. When an Anglo-Saxon named Hay Stockard and a soul-starved missionary cross his path on an unknown trail, Baptiste promises the Anglo-Saxon freedom for the cleric. But Stockard defies this heathen. And that means . . .

Brutish Beasts like Baptiste the Red and Black Leclère, however, pale compared with Wolf Larsen, London's most maniacal madman. *The Nation* charged in their 1904 review of *The Sea Wolf* that "never has sickening brutality been more gloatingly described than in this story."

The satanic Larsen loves to torture crewmen:

He crushes their heads like egg shells, bloodies their bodies, and reduces them to whining wrecks. "I believe that life is a mess," he snarls. "It is like yeast, a ferment, a thing that moves and may move for a minute, an hour, a year, or a hundred years, but that in the end will cease to move. The big eat the little that they may continue to move, the strong eat the weak that they may retain their strength. The lucky eat the most and move the longest." Larsen, of course, plays London's mouthpiece.

One of the most sadistic chapters in *The Sea Wolf* involves the Cockney cook Mugridge, whom Larsen throws overboard with a towline "for what promised sport." The fin of a man-eating shark, however, upsets this "man-play." The rest is pure horror.

These *13 Tales of Terror* explore Jack London's wicked wisdom and the unconscious threads of his soul's sickness. Maxwell Geismar calls his career "demonical in essence," his characters "victims of obsessions, delusions and grotesque missions of self-destructions," and himself "a species of devil-worshipper invoking forces of darkness which ruled a cosmos of death."

Tremble at these stories about man, London's "monstrous spectre," that "disease of the agglutinated dust." But keep the lights lit. They reveal the darkest of dark deeds.

Syracuse, New York
March 28, 1977

A THOUSAND DEATHS

I had been in the water about an hour, and cold, exhausted, with a terrible cramp in my right calf, it seemed as though my hour had come. Fruitlessly struggling against the strong ebb tide, I had beheld the maddening procession of the water-front lights slip by; but now I gave up attempting to breast the stream and contented myself with the bitter thoughts of a wasted career, now drawing to a close.

It had been my luck to come of good, English stock, but of parents whose account with the bankers far exceeded their knowledge of child-nature and the rearing of children. While born with a silver spoon in my mouth, the blessed atmosphere of the home circle was to me unknown. My father, a very learned man and a celebrated antiquarian, gave no thought to his family, being constantly lost in the abstractions of his study; while my mother, noted far more for her good looks than her good sense, sated herself with the adulation of the society in which she was perpetually plunged. I went through the regular school and college routine of a boy of the English bourgeois, and as the years brought me increasing strength and passions, my parents suddenly became aware that I was possessed of an immortal soul, and endeavored to draw the curb. But it was too late; I perpetrated the wildest and most audacious folly, and was disowned by my people, ostracized by the society I had so long outraged, and with the thousand pounds my father gave me, with the declaration that he would neither see me again nor give me more, I took a first-class passage to Australia.

Since then my life had been one long peregrination—from the Orient to the Occident, from the Arctic to the Antarctic—to find myself at last, an able seaman at thirty, in the full vigor of my manhood, drowning in San Francisco Bay because of a disastrously successful attempt to desert my ship.

My right leg was drawn up by the cramp, and I was suffering the keenest agony. A slight breeze stirred up a choppy sea, which washed into my mouth and down my throat, nor could I prevent it. Though I still contrived to keep afloat, it was merely mechanical, for I was rapidly becoming unconscious. I have a dim recollection of drifting past the sea-wall, and of catching a glimpse of an up-river steamer's starboard light; then everything became a blank.

* * * * *

I heard the low hum of insect life, and felt the balmy air of a spring morning fanning my cheek. Gradually it assumed a rhythmic flow, to whose soft pulsations my body seemed to respond. I floated on the gentle bosom of a summer's sea, rising and falling with dreamy pleasure on each crooning wave. But the pulsations grew stronger; the humming louder; the waves, larger, fiercer—I was dashed about on a stormy sea. A great agony fastened upon me. Brilliant, intermittent sparks of light flashed athwart my inner consciousness; in my ears there was the sound of many waters; then a sudden snapping of an intangible something, and I awoke.

The scene, of which I was protagonist, was a curious one. A glance sufficed to inform me that I lay on the cabin floor of some gentleman's yacht, in a most uncomfortable posture. On either side, grasping my arms and working them up and down like pump handles, were two peculiarly clad, dark-skinned creatures. Though conversant with most aboriginal types, I could not conjecture their nationality. Some attachment had been fastened about my head, which connected my respiratory organs with the machine I shall next describe. My nostrils, however, had been closed, forcing me to breathe through the mouth. Foreshortened by the obliquity of my line of vision, I beheld two tubes, similar to small hosing but of different composition, which emerged from my mouth and went off at an acute angle from each other. The first came to an abrupt termination and lay on the floor beside me; the second traversed the floor in numerous coils, connecting with the apparatus I have promised to describe.

In the days before my life had become tangential, I had dabbled not a little in science, and conversant with the appurtenances and general paraphernalia of the laboratory, I appreciated the machine I now beheld. It was composed chiefly of glass, the construction being of that crude sort which is employed for experimentative purposes. A vessel of water was surrounded by an air chamber, to which was fixed a vertical tube, surmounted by a globe. In the center of this was a vacuum gauge. The water in the tube moved upward and downward, creating alternate inhalations and exhalations, which were in turn communicated to me through the hose. With this, and the aid of the men who pumped my arms so vigorously, had the process of breathing been artificially carried on, my chest rising and falling and my lungs expanding and contracting, till nature could be persuaded to again take up her wonted labor.

As I opened my eyes the appliance about my head, nostrils and mouth was removed. Draining a stiff three fingers of brandy, I staggered to my feet to thank my preserver, and confronted—my father. But long years of fellowship with danger had taught me self-control, and I waited to see if he would recognize me. Not so; he saw in me no more than a runaway sailor and treated me accordingly.

Leaving me to the care of the blackies, he fell to revising the notes he had made on my resuscitation. As I ate of the handsome fare served up to me, confusion began on deck, and from the chanteys of the sailors and the rattling of blocks and tackles I surmised that we were getting under way. What a lark! Off on a cruise with my recluse father into the wide Pacific! Little did I realize, as I laughed to myself, which side the joke was to be on. Aye, had I known, I would have plunged overboard and welcomed the dirty fo'c'sle from which I had just escaped.

I was not allowed on deck till we had sunk the Farallones and the last pilot boat. I appreciated this forethought on the part of my father and made it a point to thank him heartily, in my bluff seaman's manner. I could not suspect that he had his own ends in view, in thus keeping my presence secret to all save the crew. He told me briefly of my rescue by his sailors, assuring me that the obligation was on his side, as my appearance had been most opportune. He had constructed the apparatus for the vindication of a theory concerning certain biological phenomena, and had been waiting for an opportunity to use it.

"You have proved it beyond all doubt," he said; then added with a sigh, "But only in the small matter of drowning."

But, to take a reef in my yarn—he offered me an advance of two pounds on my previous wages to sail with him and this I considered handsome, for he really did not need me. Contrary to my expectations, I did not join the sailors' mess, for'ard, being assigned to a comfortable stateroom and eating at the captain's table. He had perceived that I was no common sailor, and I resolved to take this chance for reinstating myself in his good graces. I wove a fic-

titious past to account for my education and
present position, and did my best to come in
touch with him. I was not long in disclosing a
predilection for scientific pursuits, nor he in ap-
preciating my aptitude. I became his assistant,
with a corresponding increase in wages, and
before long, as he grew confidential and ex-
pounded his theories, I was as enthusiastic as
himself.

The days flew quickly by, for I was deeply interested in my new studies, passing my waking
hours in his well-stocked library, or listening to
his plans and aiding him in his laboratory work.
But we were forced to forgo many enticing experiments, a rolling ship not being exactly the
proper place for delicate or intricate work. He
promised me, however, many delightful hours
in the magnificent laboratory for which we were
bound. He had taken possession of an uncharted
South Sea island, as he said, and turned it into
a scientific paradise.

We had not been on the island long, before I
discovered the horrible mare's nest I had fallen
into. But before I describe the strange things
which came to pass, I must briefly outline the
causes which culminated in as startling an experience as ever fell to the lot of man.

Late in life, my father had abandoned the
musty charms of antiquity and succumbed to
the more fascinating ones embraced under the
general head of biology. Having been thoroughly grounded during his youth in the funda-
mentals, he rapidly explored all the higher
branches as far as the scientific world had gone,

and found himself on the no man's land of the unknowable. It was his intention to pre-empt some of this unclaimed territory, and it was at this stage of his investigations that we had been thrown together. Having a good brain, though I say it myself, I had mastered his speculations and methods of reasoning, becoming almost as mad as himself. But I should not say this. The marvelous results we afterward obtained can only go to prove his sanity. I can but say that he was the most abnormal specimen of cold-blooded cruelty I have ever seen.

After having penetrated the dual mysteries of physiology and psychology, his thought had led him to the verge of a great field, for which, the better to explore, he began studies in higher organic chemistry, pathology, toxicology and other sciences and sub-sciences rendered kindred as accessories to his speculative hypotheses. Starting from the proposition that the direct cause of the temporary and permanent arrest of vitality was due to the coagulation of certain elements and compounds in the protoplasm, he had isolated and subjected these various substances to innumerable experiments. Since the temporary arrest of vitality in an organism brought coma, and a permanent arrest death, he held that by artificial means this coagulation of the protoplasm could be retarded, prevented, and even overcome in the extreme states of solidification. Or, to do away with the technical nomenclature, he argued that death, when not violent and in which none of the organs had suffered injury, was merely suspended

vitality; and that, in such instances, life could
be induced to resume its functions by the use of
proper methods. This, then, was his idea: To
discover the method—and by practical experi-
mentation prove the possibility—of renewing vitality in a structure from which life had
seemingly fled. Of course, he recognized the futility of such endeavor after decomposition had
set in; he must have organisms which but the
moment, the hour, or the day before, had been
quick with life. With me, in a crude way, he
had proved this theory. I was really drowned,
really dead, when picked from the water of San
Francisco Bay—but the vital spark had been
renewed by means of his aerotherapeutical apparatus, as he called it.

Now to his dark purpose concerning me. He
first showed me how completely I was in his
power. He had sent the yacht away for a year,
retaining only his two blackies, who were utterly devoted to him. He then made an ex-
haustive review of his theory and outlined the
method of proof he had adopted, concluding
with the startling announcement that I was to
be his subject.

I had faced death and weighed my chances
in many a desperate venture, but never in one
of this nature. I can swear I am no coward, yet
this proposition of journeying back and forth
across the borderland of death put the yellow
fear upon me. I asked for time, which he
granted, at the same time assuring me that but
the one course was open—I must submit. Escape from the island was out of the question; es-

cape by suicide was not to be entertained, though really preferable to what it seemed I must undergo; my only hope was to destroy my captors. But this latter was frustrated through the precautions taken by my father. I was subjected to a constant surveillance, even in my sleep being guarded by one or the other of the blacks.

Having pleaded in vain, I announced and proved that I was his son. It was my last card, and I had placed all my hopes upon it. But he was inexorable; he was not a father but a scientific machine. I wonder yet how it ever came to pass that he married my mother or begat me, for there was not the slightest grain of emotion in his make-up. Reason was all in all to him, nor could he understand such things as love or sympathy in others, except as petty weaknesses which should be overcome. So he informed me that in the beginning he had given me life, and who had better right to take it away than he? Such, he said, was not his desire, however; he merely wished to borrow it occasionally, promising to return it punctually at the appointed time. Of course, there was a liability of mishaps, but I could do no more than take the chances, since the affairs of men were full of such.

The better to insure success, he wished me to be in the best possible condition, so I was dieted and trained like a great athlete before a decisive contest. What could I do? If I had to undergo the peril, it were best to be in good shape. In my intervals of relaxation he allowed me to assist in the arranging of the apparatus and in the vari-

ous subsidiary experiments. The interest I took
in all such operations can be imagined. I mastered the work as thoroughly as he, and often
had the pleasure of seeing some of my sugges-
tions or alterations put into effect. After such
events I would smile grimly, conscious of of-
ficiating at my own funeral.

He began by inaugurating a series of experiments in toxicology. When all was ready, I was
killed by a stiff dose of strychnine and allowed
to lie dead for some twenty hours. During that
period my body was dead, absolutely dead. All
respiration and circulation ceased; but the
frightful part of it was, that while the protoplas-
mic coagulation proceeded, I retained consciousness and was enabled to study it in all its
ghastly details.

The apparatus to bring me back to life was
an air-tight chamber, fitted to receive my body.
The mechanism was simple—a few valves, a
rotary shaft and crank, and an electric motor.
When in operation, the interior atmosphere was
alternately condensed and rarefied, thus com-
municating to my lungs an artificial respiration
without the agency of the hosing previously
used. Though my body was inert, and, for all I
knew, in the first stages of decomposition, I was
cognizant of everything that transpired. I knew
when they placed me in the chamber, and
though all my senses were quiescent, I was
aware of the hypodermic injections of a com-
pound to react upon the coagulatory process.
Then the chamber was closed and the machinery
started. My anxiety was terrible; but the circu-

lation became gradually restored, the different organs began to carry on their respective functions, and in an hour's time I was eating a hearty dinner.

It cannot be said that I participated in this series, nor in the subsequent ones, with much verve; but after two ineffectual attempts at escape, I began to take quite an interest. Besides, I was becoming accustomed. My father was beside himself at his success, and as the months rolled by his speculations took wilder and yet wilder flights. We ranged through the three great classes of poisons, the neurotics, the gaseous and the irritants, but carefully avoided some of the mineral irritants and passed the whole group of corrosives. During the poison regime I became quite accustomed to dying, and had but one mishap to shake my growing confidence. Scarifying a number of lesser blood vessels in my arm, he introduced a minute quantity of that most frightful of poisons, the arrow poison, or curare. I lost consciousness at the start, quickly followed by the cessation of respiration and circulation, and so far had the solidification of the protoplasm advanced, that he gave up all hope. But at the last moment he applied a discovery he had been working upon, receiving such encouragement as to redouble his efforts.

In a glass vacuum, similar but not exactly like a Crookes' tube, was placed a magnetic field. When penetrated by polarized light, it gave no phenomena of phosphorescence nor of rectilinear projection of atoms, but emitted non-luminous rays, similar to the X ray. While the X ray could reveal opaque objects hidden in dense mediums, this was possessed of far subtler penetration. By this he photographed my body, and found on the negative an infinite number of blurred shadows, due to the chemical and electric motions still going on. This was an infallible proof that the rigor mortis in which I lay was not genuine; that is, those mysterious forces, those delicate bonds which held my soul to my body, were still in action. The resultants of all other poisons were unapparent, save those of mercurial compounds, which usually left me languid for several days.

Another series of delightful experiments was with electricity. We verified Tesla's assertion that high currents were utterly harmless by passing 100,000 volts through my body. As this did not affect me, the current was reduced to 2,500, and I was quickly electrocuted. This time he ventured so far as to allow me to remain dead, or in a state of suspended vitality, for three days. It took four hours to bring me back.

Once, he superinduced lockjaw, but the agony of dying was so great that I positively refused to undergo similar experiments. The easiest deaths were by asphyxiation, such as drowning, strangling, and suffocation by gas; while those by morphine, opium, cocaine and chloroform, were not at all hard.

Another time, after being suffocated, he kept me in cold storage for three months, not permitting me to freeze or decay. This was without my knowledge, and I was in a great fright on discovering the lapse of time. I became afraid of what he might do with me when I lay dead, my alarm being increased by the predilection he was beginning to betray toward vivisection. The last time I was resurrected, I discovered that he had been tampering with my breast. Though he had carefully dressed and sewed the incisions up, they were so severe that I had to take to my bed for some time. It was during this convalescence that I evolved the plan by which I ultimately escaped.

While feigning unbounded enthusiasm in the work, I asked and received a vacation from my moribund occupation. During this period I devoted myself to laboratory work, while he was too deep in the vivisection of the many animals captured by the blacks to take notice of my work.

It was on these two propositions that I constructed my theory: First, electrolysis, or the decomposition of water into its constituent gases by means of electricity; and, second, by the hypothetical existence of a force, the converse of gravitation, which Astor has named "apergy." Terrestrial attraction, for instance, merely draws objects together but does not combine them; hence, apergy is merely repulsion. Now, atomic or molecular attraction not only draws objects together but integrates them; and it was the converse of this, or a disintegrative force, which I wished to not only discover and produce, but to direct at will. Thus the molecules of hydrogen and oxygen reacting on each other, separate and create new molecules, containing both elements and forming water. Electrolysis causes these molecules to split up and resume their original condition, producing the two gases separately. The force I wished to find must not only do this with two, but with all elements, no matter in what compounds they exist. If I could then entice my father within its radius, he would be instantly disintegrated and sent flying to the four quarters, a mass of isolated elements.

It must not be understood that this force, which I finally came to control, annihilated matter, it merely annihilated form. Nor, as I soon discovered, had it any effect on inorganic structure; but to all organic form it was absolutely fatal. This partiality puzzled me at first, though had I stopped to think deeper I would have seen through it. Since the number of atoms in organic molecules is far greater than in the most complex mineral molecules, organic compounds are characterized by their instability and the ease with which they are split up by physical forces and chemical reagents.

By two powerful batteries, connected with magnets constructed specially for this purpose, two tremendous forces were projected. Considered apart from each other, they were perfectly harmless; but they accomplished their purpose by focusing at an invisible point in mid-air. After practically demonstrating its success, besides narrowly escaping being blown into nothingness, I laid my trap. Concealing the magnets, so that their force made the whole space of my chamber doorway a field of death, and placing by my couch a button by which I could throw on the current from the storage batteries, I climbed into bed.

The blackies still guarded my sleeping quarters, one relieving the other at midnight. I turned on the current as soon as the first man arrived. Hardly had I begun to doze, when I was aroused by a sharp, metallic tinkle. There, on the mid-threshold, lay the collar of Dan, my father's St. Bernard. My keeper ran to pick it up. He disappeared like a gust of wind, his clothes falling to the floor in a heap. There was a slight whiff of ozone in the air, but since the principal gaseous components of his body were hydrogen, oxygen and nitrogen, which are equally colorless and odorless, there was no other manifestation of his departure. Yet when I shut off the current and removed the garments, I found a deposit of carbon in the form of animal charcoal; also other powders, the isolated, solid elements of his organism, such as sulphur, potassium and iron. Resetting the trap, I crawled back to bed. At midnight I got up and removed the remains of the second blacky, and then slept peacefully till morning.

I was awakened by the strident voice of my father, who was calling to me from across the laboratory. I laughed to myself. There had been no one to call him and he had overslept. I could hear him as he approached my room with the intention of rousing me, and so I sat up in bed, the better to observe his translation—perhaps apotheosis were a better term. He paused a moment at the threshold, then took the fatal step. Puff! It was like the wind sighing among the pines. He was gone. His clothes fell in a fantastic heap on the floor. Besides ozone, I noticed the faint, garlic-like odor of phosphorus. A little pile of elementary solids lay among his garments. That was all. The wide world lay before me. My captors were not.

THE WHITE SILENCE

"Carmen won't last more than a couple of days." Mason spat out a chunk of ice and surveyed the poor animal ruefully, then put her foot in his mouth and proceeded to bite out the ice which clustered cruelly between the toes.

"I never saw a dog with a highfalutin' name that ever was worth a rap," he said, as he concluded his task and shoved her aside. "They just fade away and die under the responsibility. Did ye ever see one go wrong with a sensible name like Cassiar, Siwash, or Husky? No, sir! Take a look at Shookum here, he's"—

Snap! The lean brute flashed up, the white teeth just missing Mason's throat.

"Ye will, will ye?" A shrewd clout behind the ear with the butt of the dogwhip stretched the animal in the snow, quivering softly, a yellow slaver dripping from its fangs.

"As I was saying, just look at Shookum, here—he's got the spirit. Bet ye he eats Carmen before the week's out."

"I'll bank another proposition against that," replied Malemute Kid, reversing the frozen bread placed before the fire to thaw. "We'll eat Shookum before the trip is over. What d'ye say, Ruth?"

The Indian woman settled the coffee with a piece of ice, glanced from Malemute Kid to her husband, then at the dogs, but vouchsafed no reply. It was such a palpable truism that none was necessary. Two hundred miles of unbroken trail in prospect, with a scant six days' grub for themselves and none for the dogs, could admit no other alternative. The two men and the woman grouped about the fire and began their meagre meal. The dogs lay in their harnesses, for it was a midday halt, and watched each mouthful enviously.

"No more lunches after to-day," said Malemute Kid. "And we've got to keep a close eye on the dogs,—they're getting vicious. They'd just as soon pull a fellow down as not, if they get a chance."

"And I was president of an Epworth once, and taught in the Sunday school." Having irrelevantly delivered himself of this, Mason fell into a dreamy contemplation of his steaming moccasins, but was aroused by Ruth filling his cup. "Thank God, we've got slathers of tea! I've seen it growing, down in Tennessee. What wouldn't I give for a hot corn pone just now! Never mind, Ruth; you won't starve much longer, nor wear moccasins either."

The woman threw off her gloom at this, and in her eyes welled up a great love for her white lord,—the first white man she had ever seen,—the first man whom she had known to treat a woman as something better than a mere animal or beast of burden.

"Yes, Ruth," continued her husband, having recourse to the macaronic jargon in which it was alone possible for them to understand each other; "wait till we clean up and pull for the Outside. We'll take the White Man's canoe and go to the Salt Water. Yes, bad water, rough water,—great mountains dance up and down all the time. And so big, so far, so far away,—you travel ten sleep, twenty sleep, forty sleep" (he graphically enumerated the days on his fingers), "all the time water, bad water. Then you come to great village, plenty people, just the same mosquitoes next summer. Wigwams oh, so high,—ten, twenty pines. Hi-yu skookum!"

He paused impotently, cast an appealing glance at Malemute Kid, then laboriously placed the twenty pines, end on end, by sign language. Malemute Kid smiled with cheery cynicism; but Ruth's eyes were wide with wonder, and with pleasure; for she half believed he was joking, and such condescension pleased her poor woman's heart.

"And then you step into a—a box, and pouf! up you go." He tossed his empty cup in the air by way of illustration, and as he deftly caught it, cried: "And biff! down you come. Oh, great medicine-men! You go Fort Yukon, I go Arctic City,—twenty-five sleep,—big string, all the time,—I catch him string, all the time,—I say, 'Hello, Ruth! How are ye?'—and you say, 'Is that my good husband?'—and I say 'Yes,'—and you say, 'No can bake good bread, no more soda,'—then I say, 'Look in cache, under flour; good-by.' You look and catch plenty soda. All the time you Fort Yukon, me Arctic City. Hi-yu medicine-man!"

Ruth smiled so ingenuously at the fairy story, that both men burst into laughter. A row among the dogs cut short the wonders of the Outside, and by the time the snarling combatants were separated, she had lashed the sleds and all was ready for the trail.

"Mush! Baldy! Hi! Mush on!" Mason worked his whip smartly, and as the dogs whined low in the traces, broke out the sled with the gee-pole. Ruth followed with the second team, leaving Malemute Kid, who had helped her start, to bring up the rear. Strong man, brute that he was, capable of felling an ox at a blow, he could not bear to beat the poor animals, but humored them as a dog-driver rarely does,—nay, almost wept with them in their misery.

"Come, mush on there, you poor sore-footed brutes!" he murmured, after several ineffectual attempts to start the load. But his patience was at last rewarded, and though whimpering with pain, they hastened to join their fellows.

No more conversation; the toil of the trail will not permit such extravagance. And of all deadening labors, that of the Northland trail is the worst. Happy is the man who can weather a day's travel at the price of silence, and that on a beaten track.

And of all heart-breaking labors, that of breaking trail is the worst. At every step the great webbed shoe sinks till the snow is level with the knee. Then up, straight up, the deviation of a fraction of an inch being a certain precursor of disaster, the snowshoe must be lifted till the surface is cleared; then forward, down, and the other foot is raised perpendicularly for the matter of half a yard. He who tries this for the first time, if haply he avoids bringing his shoes in dangerous propinquity and measures not his length on the treacherous footing, will give up exhausted at the end of a hundred yards; he who can keep out of the way of the dogs for a whole day may well crawl into his sleeping-bag with a clear conscience and a pride which passeth all understanding; and he who travels twenty sleeps on the Long Trail is a man whom the gods may envy.

The afternoon wore on, and with the awe, born of the White Silence, the voiceless travelers bent to their work. Nature has many tricks wherewith she convinces man of his finity,—the ceaseless flow of the tides, the fury of the storm, the shock of the earthquake, the long roll of heaven's artillery,—but the most tremendous, the most stupefying of all, is the passive phase of the White Silence. All movement ceases, the sky clears, the heavens are as brass; the slightest whisper seems sacrilege, and man becomes timid, affrighted at the sound of his own voice. Sole speck of life journeying across the ghostly wastes of a dead world, he trembles at his audacity, realizes that this is a maggot's life, nothing more. Strange thoughts arise unsummoned, and the mystery of all things strives for utterance. And the fear of death, of God, of the universe, comes over him,—the hope of the Resurrection and the Life, the yearning for immortality, the vain striving of the imprisoned essence,—it is then, if ever, man walks alone with God.

So wore the day away. The river took a great bend, and Mason headed his team for the cut-off across the narrow neck of land. But the dogs balked at the high bank. Again and again, though Ruth and Malemute Kid were shoving on the sled, they slipped back. Then came the concerted effort. The miserable creatures, weak from hunger, exerted their last strength. Up—up—the sled poised on the top of the bank; but the leader swung the string of dogs behind him to the right, fouling Mason's snowshoes. The result was grievous. Mason was whipped off his feet; one of the dogs fell in the traces; and the sled toppled back, dragging everything to the bottom again.

Slash! the whip fell among the dogs savagely, especially upon the one which had fallen.

"Don't, Mason," entreated Malemute Kid; "the poor devil's on its last legs. Wait and we'll put my team on."

Mason deliberately withheld the whip till the last word had fallen, then out flashed the long lash, completely curling about the offending creature's body. Carmen—for it was Carmen—cowered in the snow, cried piteously, then rolled on her side.

It was a tragic moment, a pitiful incident of the trail,—a dying dog, two comrades in anger.

Ruth glanced solicitously from man to man. But Malemute Kid restrained himself, though there was a world of reproach in his eyes, and bending over the dog, cut the traces. No word was spoken. The teams were double-spanned and the difficulty overcome; the sleds were under way again, the dying dog dragging herself along in the rear. As long as an animal can travel, it is not shot, and this last chance is accorded it,— the crawling into camp, if it can, in the hope of a moose being killed.

Already penitent for his angry action, but too stubborn to make amends, Mason toiled on at the head of the cavalcade, little dreaming that danger hovered in the air. The timber clustered thick in the sheltered bottom, and through this they threaded their way. Fifty feet or more from the trail towered a lofty pine. For generations it had stood there, and for generations destiny had had this one end in view,—perhaps the same had been decreed of Mason.

He stooped to fasten the loosened thong of his moccasin. The sleds came to a halt and the dogs lay down in the snow without a whimper. The stillness was weird; not a breath rustled the frost-encrusted forest; the cold and silence of outer space had chilled the heart and smote the trembling lips of nature. A sigh pulsed through the air,—they did not seem to actually hear it, but rather felt it, like the premonition of movement in a motionless void. Then the great tree, burdened with its weight of years and snow, played its last part in the tragedy of life. He heard the warning crash and attempted to spring up, but almost erect, caught the blow squarely on the shoulder.

The sudden danger, the quick death,—how often had Malemute Kid faced it! The pine needles were still quivering as he gave his commands and sprang into action. Nor did the Indian girl faint or raise her voice in idle wailing, as might many of her white sisters. At his order, she threw her weight on the end of a quickly extemporized handspike, easing the pressure and listening to her husband's groans, while Malemute Kid attacked the tree with his axe. The steel rang merrily as it bit into the frozen trunk, each stroke being accompanied by a forced, audible respiration, the "Huh!" "Huh!" of the woodsman.

At last the Kid laid the pitiable thing that was once a man in the snow. But worse than his comrade's pain was the dumb anguish in the woman's face, the blended look of hopeful, hopeless query. Little was said; those of the Northland are early taught the futility of words and the inestimable value of deeds. With the temperature at sixty-five below zero, a man cannot lie many minutes in the snow and live. So the sled-lashings were cut, and the sufferer, rolled in furs, laid on a couch of boughs. Before him roared a fire, built of the very wood which wrought the mishap. Behind and partially over him was stretched the primitive fly,—a piece of canvas, which caught the radiating heat and threw it back and down upon him,—a trick which men may know who study physics at the fount.

And men who have shared their bed with death know when the call is sounded. Mason was terribly crushed. The most cursory examination revealed it. His right arm, leg, and back, were broken; his limbs were paralyzed from the hips; and the likelihood of internal injuries was large. An occasional moan was his only sign of life.

No hope; nothing to be done. The pitiless night crept slowly by,—Ruth's portion, the despairing stoicism of her race, and Malemute Kid adding new lines to his face of bronze. In fact, Mason suffered the least of all, for he spent his time in Eastern Tennessee, in the Great Smoky Mountains, living over the scenes of his childhood. And most pathetic was the melody of his long-forgotten Southern vernacular, as he raved of swimming-holes and coon-hunts and watermelon raids. It was as Greek to Ruth, but the Kid understood and felt,—felt as only one can feel who has been shut out for years from all that civilization means.

Morning brought consciousness to the stricken man, and Malemute Kid bent closer to catch his whispers.

"You remember when we foregathered on the Tanana, four years come next ice-run? I didn't care so much for her then. It was more like she was pretty, and there was a smack of excitement about it, I think. But d' ye know, I've come to think a heap of her. She's been a good wife to me, always at my shoulder in the pinch. And when it comes to trading, you know there isn't her equal. D' ye recollect the time she shot the

Moosehorn Rapids to pull you and me off that rock, the bullets whipping the water like hailstones?—and the time of the famine at Nuklukyeto?—or when she raced the ice-run to bring the news? Yes, she's been a good wife to me, better 'n that other one. Didn't know I'd been there? Never told you, eh? Well, I tried it once, down in the States. That's why I'm here. Been raised together, too. I came away to give her a chance for divorce. She got it.

"But that's got nothing to do with Ruth. I had thought of cleaning up and pulling for the Outside next year,—her and I,—but it's too late. Don't send her back to her people, Kid. It's beastly hard for a woman to go back. Think of it!—nearly four years on our bacon and beans and flour and dried fruit, and then to go back to her fish and cariboo. It's not good for her to have tried our ways, to come to know they're better 'n her people's, and then return to them. Take care of her, Kid,—why don't you,—but no, you always fought shy of them,—and you never told me why you came to this country. Be kind to her, and send her back to the States as soon as you can. But fix it so as she can come back,— liable to get homesick, you know.

"And the youngster—it's drawn us closer, Kid. I only hope it is a boy. Think of it!—flesh of my flesh, Kid. He mustn't stop in this country. And if it's a girl, why she can't. Sell my furs; they'll fetch at least five thousand, and I've got as much more with the company. And handle my interests with yours. I think that bench claim will show up. See that he gets a good schooling;

and Kid, above all, don't let him come back. This country was not made for white men.

"I'm a gone man, Kid. Three or four sleeps at the best. You've got to go on. You must go on! Remember, it's my wife, it's my boy,—O God! I hope it's a boy! You can't stay by me,—and I charge you, a dying man, to pull on."

"Give me three days," pleaded Malemute Kid. "You may change for the better; something may turn up."

"No."

"Just three days."

"You must pull on."

"Two days."

"It's my wife and my boy, Kid. You would not ask it."

"One day."

"No, no! I charge"—

"Only one day. We can shave it through on the grub, and I might knock over a moose."

"No,—all right; one day, but not a minute more. And Kid, don't—don't leave me to face it alone. Just a shot, one pull on the trigger. You understand. Think of it! Think of it! Flesh of my flesh, and I'll never live to see him!

"Send Ruth here. I want to say good-by and tell her that she must think of the boy and not wait till I'm dead. She might refuse to go with you if I didn't. Good-by, old man; good-by.

"Kid! I say—a—sink a hole above the pup, next to the slide. I panned out forty cents on my shovel there.

"And Kid!" he stooped lower to catch the last

faint words, the dying man's surrender of his
pride. "I'm sorry—for—you know—Carmen."

Leaving the girl crying softly over her man,
Malemute Kid slipped into his *parka* and snow-
shoes, tucked his rifle under his arm, and crept
away into the forest. He was no tyro in the stern
sorrows of the Northland, but never had he
faced so stiff a problem as this. In the abstract,
it was a plain, mathematical proposition,—three
possible lives as against one doomed one. But
now he hesitated. For five years, shoulder to
shoulder, on the rivers and trails, in the camps
and mines, facing death by field and flood and
famine, had they knitted the bonds of their
comradeship. So close was the tie, that he had
often been conscious of a vague jealousy of
Ruth, from the first time she had come between.
And now it must be severed by his own hand.

Though he prayed for a moose, just one
moose, all game seemed to have deserted the
land, and nightfall found the exhausted man
crawling into camp, light-handed, heavy-
hearted. An uproar from the dogs and shrill
cries from Ruth hastened him.

Bursting into the camp, he saw the girl in the
midst of the snarling pack, laying about her
with an axe. The dogs had broken the iron rule
of their masters and were rushing the grub. He
joined the issue with his rifle reversed, and the
hoary game of natural selection was played out
with all the ruthlessness of its primeval environment. Rifle and axe went up and down, hit or
missed with monotonous regularity; lithe bodies
flashed, with wild eyes and dripping fangs; and

man and beast fought for supremacy to the bitterest conclusion. Then the beaten brutes crept to the edge of the firelight, licking their wounds, voicing their misery to the stars.

The whole stock of dried salmon had been devoured, and perhaps five pounds of flour remained to tide them over two hundred miles of wilderness. Ruth returned to her husband, while Malemute Kid cut up the warm body of one of the dogs, the skull of which had been crushed by the axe. Every portion was carefully put away, save the hide and offal, which were cast to his fellows of the moment before.

Morning brought fresh trouble. The animals were turning on each other. Carmen, who still clung to her slender thread of life, was downed by the pack. The lash fell among them unheeded. They cringed and cried under the blows, but refused to scatter till the last wretched bit had disappeared,—bones, hide, hair, everything.

Malemute Kid went about his work, listening to Mason, who was back in Tennessee, delivering tangled discourses and wild exhortations to his brethren of other days.

Taking advantage of neighboring pines, he worked rapidly, and Ruth watched him make a cache similar to those sometimes used by hunters to preserve their meat from the wolverines and dogs. One after the other, he bent the tops of two small pines toward each other and nearly to the ground, making them fast with thongs of moosehide. Then he beat the dogs into submission and harnessed them to two of

the sleds, loading the same with everything but
the furs which enveloped Mason. These he
wrapped and lashed tightly about him, fasten-
ing either end of the robes to the bent pines. A
single stroke of his hunting-knife would release
them and send the body high in the air.

Ruth had received her husband's last wishes
and made no struggle. Poor girl, she had
learned the lesson of obedience well. From a
child, she had bowed, and seen all women bow,
to the lords of creation, and it did not seem in
the nature of things for woman to resist. The
Kid permitted her one outburst of grief, as she
kissed her husband,—her own people had no
such custom,—then led her to the foremost sled
and helped her into her snowshoes. Blindly, instinctively, she took the gee-pole and whip, and
"mushed" the dogs out on the trail. Then he returned to Mason, who had fallen into a coma;
and long after she was out of sight, crouched by
the fire, waiting, hoping, praying for his comrade to die.

It is not pleasant to be alone with painful
thoughts in the White Silence. The silence of
gloom is merciful, shrouding one as with protection and breathing a thousand intangible sym-
pathies; but the bright White Silence, clear and
cold, under steely skies, is pitiless.

An hour passed,—two hours,—but the man
would not die. At high noon, the sun, without
raising its rim above the southern horizon,
threw a suggestion of fire athwart the heavens,
then quickly drew it back. Malemute Kid
roused and dragged himself to his comrade's

side. He cast one glance about him. The White Silence seemed to sneer, and a great fear came upon him. There was a sharp report; Mason swung into his aerial sepulchre; and Malemute Kid lashed the dogs into a wild gallop as he fled across the snow.

IN A FAR COUNTRY

When a man journeys into a far country, he must be prepared to forget many of the things he has learned, and to acquire such customs as are inherent with existence in the new land; he must abandon the old ideals and the old gods, and oftentimes he must reverse the very codes by which his conduct has hitherto been shaped. To those who have the protean faculty of adaptability, the novelty of such change may even be a source of pleasure; but to those who happen to be hardened to the ruts in which they were created, the pressure of the altered environment is unbearable, and they chafe in body and in spirit under the new restrictions which they do not understand. This chafing is bound to act and react, producing divers evils and leading to various misfortunes. It were better for the man who cannot fit himself to the new groove to return to his own country; if he delay too long, he will surely die.

The man who turns his back upon the comforts of an elder civilization, to face the savage youth, the primordial simplicity of the North, may estimate success at an inverse ratio to the quantity and quality of his hopelessly fixed habits. He will soon discover, if he be a fit candidate, that the material habits are the less important. The exchange of such things as a dainty menu for rough fare, of the stiff leather shoe for the soft, shapeless moccasin, of the feather bed for a couch in the snow, is after all a very easy matter. But his pinch will come in learning properly to shape his mind's attitude toward all things, and especially toward his fellow man. For the courtesies of ordinary life, he must substitute unselfishness, forbearance, and tolerance. Thus, and thus only, can he gain that pearl of great price,—true comradeship. He must not say "Thank you;" he must mean it without opening his mouth, and prove it by responding in kind. In short, he must substitute the deed for the word, the spirit for the letter.

When the world rang with the tale of Arctic gold, and the lure of the North gripped the heartstrings of men, Carter Weatherbee threw up his snug clerkship, turned the half of his savings over to his wife, and with the remainder bought an outfit. There was no romance in his nature,—the bondage of commerce had crushed all that; he was simply tired of the ceaseless grind, and wished to risk great hazards in view of corresponding returns. Like many another fool, disdaining the old trails used by the Northland pioneers for a score of years, he hurried to Edmonton in the spring of the year; and there, unluckily for his soul's welfare, he allied himself with a party of men.

There was nothing unusual about this party,

except its plans. Even its goal, like that of all other parties, was the Klondike. But the route it had mapped out to attain that goal took away the breath of the hardiest native, born and bred to the vicissitudes of the Northwest. Even Jacques Baptiste, born of a Chippewa woman and a renegade *voyageur* (having raised his first whimpers in a deerskin lodge north of the sixty-fifth parallel, and had the same hushed by blissful sucks of raw tallow), was surprised. Though he sold his services to them and agreed to travel even to the never-opening ice, he shook his head ominously whenever his advice was asked.

Percy Cuthfert's evil star must have been in the ascendant, for he, too, joined this company of argonauts. He was an ordinary man, with a bank account as deep as his culture, which is saying a good deal. He had no reason to embark on such a venture,—no reason in the world, save that he suffered from an abnormal development of sentimentality. He mistook this for the true spirit of romance and adventure. Many another man has done the like, and made as fatal a mistake.

The first break-up of spring found the party following the ice-run of Elk River. It was an imposing fleet, for the outfit was large, and they were accompanied by a disreputable contingent of half-breed *voyageurs* with their women and children. Day in and day out, they labored with the bateaux and canoes, fought mosquitoes and other kindred pests, or sweated and swore at the portages. Severe toil like this lays a man naked to the very roots of his soul, and ere Lake

Athabasca was lost in the south, each member of the party had hoisted his true colors.

The two shirks and chronic grumblers were Carter Weatherbee and Percy Cuthfert. The whole party complained less of its aches and pains than did either of them. Not once did they volunteer for the thousand and one petty duties of the camp. A bucket of water to be brought, an extra armful of wood to be chopped, the dishes to be washed and wiped, a search to be made through the outfit for some suddenly indispensable article,—and these two effete scions of civilization discovered sprains or blisters requiring instant attention. They were the first to turn in at night, with a score of tasks yet undone; the last to turn out in the morning, when the start should be in readiness before the breakfast was begun. They were the first to fall to at meal-time, the last to have a hand in the cooking; the first to dive for a slim delicacy, the last to discover they had added to their own another man's share. If they toiled at the oars, they slyly cut the water at each stroke and allowed the boat's momentum to float up the blade. They thought nobody noticed; but their comrades swore under their breaths and grew to hate them, while Jacques Baptiste sneered openly and damned them from morning till night. But Jacques Baptiste was no gentleman.

At the Great Slave, Hudson Bay dogs were purchased, and the fleet sank to the guards with its added burden of dried fish and pemmican. Then canoe and bateau answered to the swift current of the Mackenzie, and they plunged

into the Great Barren Ground. Every likely-
looking "feeder" was prospected, but the elusive
"pay-dirt" danced over to the north. At the
Great Bear, overcome by the common dread of
the Unknown Lands, their *voyageurs* began to
desert, and Fort of Good Hope saw the last and
bravest bending to the tow-lines as they bucked
the current down which they had so treacherously glided. Jacques Baptiste alone remained.
Had he not sworn to travel even to the never-
opening ice?

The lying charts, compiled in main from
hearsay, were not instantly consulted. And
they felt the need of hurry, for the sun had
already passed its northern solstice and was
leading the winter south again. Skirting the
shores of the bay, where the Mackenzie disem-
bogues into the Arctic Ocean, they entered the
mouth of the Little Peel River. Then began the
arduous upstream toil, and the two Incapables
fared worse than ever. Tow-line and pole, paddle and tump-line, rapids and portages,—such
tortures served to give the one a deep disgust
for great hazards, and printed for the other a
fiery text on the true romance of adventure. One
day they waxed mutinous, and being vilely
cursed by Jacques Baptiste, turned, as worms
sometimes will. But the half-breed thrashed the
twain, and sent them, bruised and bleeding,
about their work. It was the first time either had
been manhandled.

Abandoning their river craft at the head-
waters of the Little Peel, they consumed the rest
of the summer in the great portage over the

Mackenzie watershed to the West Rat. This
little stream fed the Porcupine, which in turn
joined the Yukon where that mighty highway of
the North countermarches on the Arctic Circle.
But they had lost in the race with winter, and
one day they tied their rafts to the thick eddy-
ice and hurried their goods ashore. That night
the river jammed and broke several times; the
following morning it had fallen asleep for good.

"We can't be more 'n four hundred miles
from the Yukon," concluded Sloper, multiplying
his thumb nails by the scale of the map. The
council, in which the two Incapables had
whined to excellent disadvantage, was drawing
to a close.

"Hudson Bay Post, long time ago. No use um
now." Jacques Baptiste's father had made the
trip for the Fur Company in the old days, in-
cidentally marking the trail with a couple of
frozen toes.

"Sufferin' cracky!" cried another of the party.
"No whites?"

"Nary white," Sloper sententiously affirmed;
"but it's only five hundred more up the Yukon
to Dawson. Call it a rough thousand from here.

Weatherbee and Cuthfert groaned in chorus.

"How long'll that take, Baptiste?"

The half-breed figured for a moment. "Work-
um like hell, no man play out, ten—twenty—
forty—fifty days. Um babies come" (designating
the Incapables), "no can tell. Mebbe when hell
freeze over; mebbe not then."

The manufacture of snowshoes and moccasins ceased. Somebody called the name of an absent member, who came out of an ancient cabin at the edge of the camp-fire and joined them. The cabin was one of the many mysteries which lurk in the vast recesses of the North. Built when and by whom, no man could tell. Two graves in the open, piled high with stones, perhaps contained the secret of those early wanderers. But whose hand had piled the stones?

The moment had come. Jacques Baptiste paused in the fitting of a harness and pinned the struggling dog in the snow. The cook made mute protest for delay, threw a handful of bacon into a noisy pot of beans, then came to attention. Sloper rose to his feet. His body was a ludicrous contrast to the healthy physiques of the Incapables. Yellow and weak, fleeing from a South American fever-hole, he had not broken his flight across the zones, and was still able to toil with men. His weight was probably ninety pounds, with the heavy hunting-knife thrown in, and his grizzled hair told of a prime which had ceased to be. The fresh young muscles of either Weatherbee or Cuthfert were equal to ten times the endeavor of his; yet he could walk them into the earth in a day's journey. And all this day he had whipped his stronger comrades into venturing a thousand miles of the stiffest hardship man can conceive. He was the incarnation of the unrest of his race, and the old Teutonic stubbornness, dashed with the quick grasp and action of the Yankee, held the flesh in the bondage of the spirit.

"All those in favor of going on with the dogs as soon as the ice sets, say ay."

"Ay!" rang out eight voices,—voices destined to string a trail of oaths along many a hundred miles of pain.

"Contrary minded?"

"No!" For the first time the Incapables were united without some compromise of personal interests.

"And what are you going to do about it?" Weatherbee added belligerently.

"Majority rule! Majority rule!" clamored the rest of the party.

"I know the expedition is liable to fall through if you don't come," Sloper replied sweetly; "but I guess, if we try real hard, we can manage to do without you. What do you say, boys?"

The sentiment was cheered to the echo.

"But I say, you know," Cuthfert ventured apprehensively; "what's a chap like me to do?"

"Ain't you coming with us?"

"No-o."

"Then do as you damn well please. We won't have nothing to say."

"Kind o' calkilate yuh might settle it with that canoodlin' pardner of yourn," suggested a heavy-going Westerner from the Dakotas, at the same time pointing out Weatherbee. "He'll be shore to ask yuh what yur a-goin' to do when it comes to cookin' an' gatherin' the wood."

"Then we'll consider it all arranged," concluded Sloper. "We'll pull out to-morrow, if we camp within five miles,—just to get everything in running order and remember if we've forgotten anything."

The sleds groaned by on their steel-shod runners, and the dogs strained low in the harnesses in which they were born to die. Jacques Baptiste paused by the side of Sloper to get a last glimpse of the cabin. The smoke curled up pathetically from the Yukon stove-pipe. The two Incapables were watching them from the doorway.

Sloper laid his hand on the other's shoulder.

"Jacques Baptiste, did you ever hear of the Kilkenny cats?"

The half-breed shook his head.

"Well, my friend and good comrade, the Kilkenny cats fought till neither hide, nor hair, nor yowl, was left. You understand?—till nothing was left. Very good. Now, these two men don't like work. They won't work. We know that. They'll be all alone in that cabin all winter,—a mighty long, dark winter. Kilkenny cats,—well?"

The Frenchman in Baptiste shrugged his shoulders, but the Indian in him was silent. Nevertheless, it was an eloquent shrug, pregnant with prophecy.

Things prospered in the little cabin at first. The rough badinage of their comrades had made Weatherbee and Cuthfert conscious of the mutual responsibility which had devolved upon them; besides there was not so much work after all for two healthy men. And the removal of the cruel whip-hand, or in other words the bulldozing half-breed, had brought with it a joyous reaction. At first, each strove to outdo the other, and they performed petty tasks with an unction which would have opened the eyes of their comrades who were now wearing out bodies and souls on the Long Trail.

All care was banished. The forest, which shouldered in upon them from three sides, was an inexhaustible woodyard. A few yards from their door slept the Porcupine, and a hole through its winter robe formed a bubbling spring of water, crystal clear and painfully cold. But they soon grew to find fault with even that. The hole would persist in freezing up, and thus gave them many a miserable hour of ice-chopping. The unknown builders of the cabin had extended the side-logs so as to support a cache at the rear. In this was stored the bulk of the party's provisions. Food there was, without stint, for three times the men who were fated to live upon it. But the most of it was of the kind which built up brawn and sinew, but did not tickle the palate. True, there was sugar in plenty for two ordinary men; but these two were little else than children. They early discovered the virtues of hot water judiciously saturated with sugar, and they prodigally swam their flapjacks and soaked their crusts in the rich, white syrup. Then coffee and tea, and especially the dried fruits, made disastrous inroads upon it. The first words they had were over the sugar question. And it is a really serious thing when two men, wholly dependent upon each other for company, begin to quarrel.

Weatherbee loved to discourse blatantly on politics, while Cuthfert, who had been prone to clip his coupons and let the commonwealth jog on as best it might, either ignored the subject or delivered himself of startling epigrams. But the clerk was too obtuse to appreciate the clever shaping of thought, and this waste of ammunition irritated Cuthfert. He had been used to blinding people by his brilliancy, and it worked him quite a hardship, this loss of an audience. He felt personally aggrieved and unconsciously held his mutton-head companion responsible for it.

Save existence, they had nothing in common,—came in touch on no single point. Weatherbee was a clerk who had known naught but clerking all his life; Cuthfert was a master of arts, a dabbler in oils, and had written not a little. The one was a lower-class man who considered himself a gentleman, and the other was a gentleman who knew himself to be such. From this it may be remarked that a man can be a gentleman without possessing the first instinct of true comradeship. The clerk was as sensuous as the other was aesthetic, and his love adventures, told at great length and chiefly coined from his imagination, affected the supersensitive master of arts in the same way as so many whiffs of sewer gas. He deemed the clerk a filthy, uncultured brute, whose place was in the muck with the swine, and told him so; and he was reciprocally informed that he was a milk-and-water sissy and a cad. Weatherbee could not have defined "cad" for his life; but it satisfied its

purpose, which after all seems the main point in
life.

Weatherbee flatted every third note and sang
such songs as "The Boston Burglar" and "The
Handsome Cabin Boy," for hours at a time,
while Cuthfert wept with rage, till he could
stand it no longer and fled into the outer cold.
But there was no escape. The intense frost could
not be endured for long at a time, and the little
cabin crowded them—beds, stove, table, and
all—into a space of ten by twelve. The very
presence of either became a personal affront to
the other, and they lapsed into sullen silences
which increased in length and strength as the
days went by. Occasionally, the flash of an eye
or the curl of a lip got the better of them,
though they strove to wholly ignore each other
during these mute periods. And a great wonder
sprang up in the breast of each, as to how God
had ever come to create the other.

With little to do, time became an intolerable
burden to them. This naturally made them still
lazier. They sank into a physical lethargy which
there was no escaping, and which made them
rebel at the performance of the smallest chore.
One morning when it was his turn to cook the
common breakfast, Weatherbee rolled out of his
blankets, and to the snoring of his companion,
lighted first the slush-lamp and then the fire.
The kettles were frozen hard, and there was no
water in the cabin with which to wash. But he
did not mind that. Waiting for it to thaw, he
sliced the bacon and plunged into the hateful
task of bread-making. Cuthfert had been slyly

watching through his half-closed lids. Consequently there was a scene, in which they fervently blessed each other, and agreed, thenceforth, that each do his own cooking. A week later, Cuthfert neglected his morning ablutions, but none the less complacently ate the meal which he had cooked. Weatherbee grinned. After that the foolish custom of washing passed out of their lives.

As the sugar-pile and other little luxuries dwindled, they began to be afraid they were not getting their proper shares, and in order that they might not be robbed, they fell to gorging themselves. The luxuries suffered in this gluttonous contest, as did also the men. In the absence of fresh vegetables and exercise, their blood became impoverished, and a loathsome, purplish rash crept over their bodies. Yet they refused to heed the warning. Next, their muscles and joints began to swell, the flesh turning black, while their mouths, gums, and lips took on the color of rich cream. Instead of being drawn together by their misery, each gloated over the other's symptoms as the scurvy took its course.

They lost all regard for personal appearance, and for that matter, common decency. The cabin became a pigpen, and never once were the beds made or fresh pine boughs laid underneath. Yet they could not keep to their blankets, as they would have wished; for the frost was inexorable, and the fire box consumed much fuel. The hair of their heads and faces grew long and shaggy, while their garments

would have disgusted a ragpicker. But they did
not care. They were sick, and there was no one
to see; besides, it was very painful to move
about.

To all this was added a new trouble,—the Fear
of the North. This Fear was the joint child of
the Great Cold and the Great Silence, and was
born in the darkness of December, when the
sun dipped below the southern horizon for
good. It affected them according to their
natures. Weatherbee fell prey to the grosser su-
perstitions, and did his best to resurrect the
spirits which slept in the forgotten graves. It
was a fascinating thing, and in his dreams they
came to him from out of the cold, and snuggled
into his blankets, and told him of their toils and
troubles ere they died. He shrank away from
the clammy contact as they drew closer and
twined their frozen limbs about him, and when
they whispered in his ear of things to come, the
cabin rang with his frightened shrieks. Cuthfert
did not understand,—for they no longer
spoke,—and when thus awakened he invariably
grabbed for his revolver. Then he would sit up
in bed, shivering nervously, with the weapon
trained on the unconscious dreamer. Cuthfert
deemed the man going mad, and so came to
fear for his life.

His own malady assumed a less concrete
form. The mysterious artisan who had laid the
cabin, log by log, had pegged a wind-vane to
the ridge-pole. Cuthfert noticed it always
pointed south, and one day, irritated by its
steadfastness of purpose, he turned it toward

the east. He watched eagerly, but never a breath came by to disturb it. Then he turned the vane to the north, swearing never again to touch it till the wind did blow. But the air frightened him with its unearthly calm, and he often rose in the middle of the night to see if the vane had veered,—ten degrees would have satisfied him. But no, it poised above him as unchangeable as fate. His imagination ran riot, till it became to him a fetish. Sometimes he followed the path it pointed across the dismal dominions, and allowed his soul to become saturated with the Fear. He dwelt upon the unseen and the unknown till the burden of eternity appeared to be crushing him. Everything in the Northland had that crushing effect,—the absence of life and motion; the darkness; the infinite peace of the brooding land; the ghastly silence, which made the echo of each heart-beat a sacrilege; the solemn forest which seemed to guard an awful inexpressible something, which neither word nor thought could compass.

The world he had so recently left, with its busy nations and great enterprises, seemed very far away. Recollections occasionally obtruded,—recollections of marts and galleries and crowded thoroughfares, of evening dress and social functions, of good men and dear women he had known,—but they were dim memories of a life he had lived long centuries agone, on some other planet. This phantasm was the Reality. Standing beneath the wind-vane, his eyes fixed on the polar skies, he could not bring himself to realize that the Southland really existed,

that at that very moment it was a-roar with life
and action. There was no Southland, no men
being born of women, no giving and taking in
marriage. Beyond his bleak sky-line there
stretched vast solitudes, and beyond these still
vaster solitudes. There were no lands of sunshine, heavy with the perfume of flowers. Such
things were only dreams of paradise. The sun-
lands of the West and the spicelands of the
East, the smiling Arcadias and blissful Islands
of the Blest,—ha! ha! His laughter split the void
and shocked him with its unwonted sound.
There was no sun. This was the Universe, dead
and cold and dark, and he its only citizen.
Weatherbee? At such moments Weatherbee did
not count. He was a Caliban, a monstrous phan-
tom, fettered to him for untold ages, the penalty
of some forgotten crime.

He lived with Death among the dead, emas-
culated by the sense of his own insignificance,
crushed by the passive mastery of the slumber-
ing ages. The magnitude of all things appalled
him. Everything partook of the superlative save
himself,—the perfect cessation of wind and motion, the immensity of the snow-covered wilderness, the height of the sky and the depth of the
silence. That wind-vane,—if it would only move.
If a thunderbolt would fall, or the forest flare
up in flame. The rolling up of the heavens as a
scroll, the crash of Doom—anything, anything!
But no, nothing moved; the Silence crowded in,
and the Fear of the North laid icy fingers on his
heart.

Once, like another Crusoe, by the edge of the

river he came upon a track,—the faint tracery of
a snowshoe rabbit on the delicate snow-crust. It
was a revelation. There was life in the Northland. He would follow it, look upon it, gloat
over it. He forgot his swollen muscles, plunging
through the deep snow in an ecstasy of anticipation. The forest swallowed him up, and the
brief midday twilight vanished; but he pursued
his quest till exhausted nature asserted itself
and laid him helpless in the snow. There he
groaned and cursed his folly, and knew the
track to be the fancy of his brain; and late that
night he dragged himself into the cabin on
hands and knees, his cheeks frozen and a
strange numbness about his feet. Weatherbee
grinned malevolently, but made no offer to help
him. He thrust needles into his toes and thawed
them out by the stove. A week later mortifica-
tion set in.

But the clerk had his own troubles. The dead
men came out of their graves more frequently
now, and rarely left him, waking or sleeping. He
grew to wait and dread their coming, never
passing the twin cairns without a shudder. One
night they came to him in his sleep and led him
forth to an appointed task. Frightened into inar-
ticulate horror, he awoke between the heaps of
stones and fled wildly to the cabin. But he had
lain there for some time, for his feet and cheeks
were also frozen.

Sometimes he became frantic at their insistent presence, and danced about the cabin, cutting the empty air with an axe, and smashing
everything within reach. During these ghostly

encounters, Cuthfert huddled into his blankets and followed the madman about with a cocked revolver, ready to shoot him if he came too near. But, recovering from one of these spells, the clerk noticed the weapon trained upon him. His suspicions were aroused, and thenceforth he, too, lived in fear of his life. They watched each other closely after that, and faced about in startled fright whenever either passed behind the other's back. This apprehensiveness became a mania which controlled them even in their sleep. Through mutual fear they tacitly let the slush-lamp burn all night, and saw to a plentiful supply of bacon-grease before retiring. The slightest movement on the part of one was sufficient to arouse the other, and many a still watch their gazes countered as they shook beneath their blankets with fingers on the trigger-guards.

What with the Fear of the North, the mental strain, and the ravages of the disease, they lost all semblance of humanity, taking on the appearance of wild beasts, hunted and desperate. Their cheeks and noses, as an aftermath of the freezing, had turned black. Their frozen toes had begun to drop away at the first and second joints. Every movement brought pain, but the fire box was insatiable, wringing a ransom of torture from their miserable bodies. Day in, day out, it demanded its food,—a veritable pound of flesh,—and they dragged themselves into the forest to chop wood on their knees. Once, crawling thus in search of dry sticks, unknown to each other they entered a thicket from opposite sides. Suddenly, without warning, two peering death's-heads confronted each other. Suffering had so transformed them that recognition was impossible. They sprang to their feet, shrieking with terror, and dashed away on their mangled stumps; and falling at the cabin door, they clawed and scratched like demons till they discovered their mistake.

Occasionally they lapsed normal, and during one of these sane intervals, the chief bone of contention, the sugar, had been divided equally between them. They guarded their separate sacks, stored up in the cache, with jealous eyes; for there were but a few cupfuls left, and they were totally devoid of faith in each other. But one day Cuthfert made a mistake. Hardly able to move, sick with pain, with his head swimming and eyes blinded, he crept into the cache, sugar canister in hand, and mistook Weatherbee's sack for his own.

January had been born but a few days when this occurred. The sun had some time since passed its lowest southern declination, and at meridian now threw flaunting streaks of yellow light upon the northern sky. On the day following his mistake with the sugarbag, Cuthfert found himself feeling better, both in body and in spirit. As noontime drew near and the day brightened, he dragged himself outside to feast on the evanescent glow, which was to him an earnest of the sun's future intentions. Weatherbee was also feeling somewhat better, and crawled out beside him. They propped themselves in the snow beneath the moveless wind-vane, and waited.

The stillness of death was about them. In other climes, when nature falls into such moods, there is a subdued air of expectancy, a waiting for some small voice to take up the broken strain. Not so in the North. The two men had lived seeming aeons in this ghostly peace. They could remember no song of the past; they could conjure no song of the future. This unearthly calm had always been,—the tranquil silence of eternity.

Their eyes were fixed upon the north. Unseen, behind their backs, behind the towering mountains to the south, the sun swept toward the zenith of another sky than theirs. Sole spectators of the mighty canvas, they watched the false dawn slowly grow. A faint flame began to glow and smoulder. It deepened in intensity, ringing the changes of reddish-yellow, purple, and saffron. So bright did it become that Cuthfert thought the sun must surely be behind it,—a miracle, the sun rising in the north! Suddenly, without warning and without fading, the canvas was swept clean. There was no color in the sky. The light had gone out of the day. They caught their breaths in half-sobs. But lo! the air was a-glint with particles of scintillating frost, and there, to the north, the wind-vane lay in vague outline on the snow. A shadow! A shadow! It was exactly midday. They jerked their heads hurriedly to the south. A golden rim peeped over the mountain's snowy shoulder,

smiled upon them an instant, then dipped from
sight again.

There were tears in their eyes as they sought
each other. A strange softening came over them.
They felt irresistibly drawn toward each other.
The sun was coming back again. It would be
with them to-morrow, and the next day, and the
next. And it would stay longer every visit, and a
time would come when it would ride their
heaven day and night, never once dropping below the sky-line. There would be no night. The
ice-locked winter would be broken; the winds
would blow and the forests answer; the land
would bathe in the blessed sunshine, and life
renew. Hand in hand, they would quit this hor-
rid dream and journey back to the Southland.
They lurched blindly forward, and their hands
met,—their poor maimed hands, swollen and dis-
torted beneath their mittens.

But the promise was destined to remain un-
fulfilled. The Northland is the Northland, and
men work out their souls by strange rules, which
other men, who have not journeyed into far
countries, cannot come to understand.

An hour later, Cuthfert put a pan of bread
into the oven, and fell to speculating on what
the surgeons could do with his feet when he got
back. Home did not seem so very far away now.
Weatherbee was rummaging in the cache. Of a
sudden, he raised a whirl-wind of blasphemy,
which in turn ceased with startling abruptness.
The other man had robbed his sugar-sack. Still,
things might have happened differently, had

not the two dead men come out from under the
stones and hushed the hot words in his throat.
They led him quite gently from the cache,
which he forgot to close. That consummation
was reached; that something they had whispered to him in his dreams was about to happen. They guided him gently, very gently, to
the woodpile, where they put the axe in his
hands. Then they helped him shove open the
cabin door, and he felt sure they shut it after
him,—at least he heard it slam and the latch
fall sharply into place. And he knew they were
waiting just without, waiting for him to do his
task.

"Carter! I say, Carter!"

Percy Cuthfert was frightened at the look on
the clerk's face, and he made haste to put the
table between them.

Carter Weatherbee followed, without haste
and without enthusiasm. There was neither pity
nor passion in his face, but rather the patient,
stolid look of one who has certain work to do
and goes about it methodically.

"I say, what's the matter?"

The clerk dodged back, cutting off his retreat
to the door, but never opening his mouth.

"I say, Carter, I say; let's talk. There's a good
chap."

The master of arts was thinking rapidly, now,
shaping a skillful flank movement on the bed
where his Smith & Wesson lay. Keeping his eyes
on the madman, he rolled backward on the
bunk, at the same time clutching the pistol.

"Carter!"

The powder flashed full in Weatherbee's face, but he swung his weapon and leaped forward. The axe bit deeply at the base of the spine, and Percy Cuthfert felt all consciousness of his lower limbs leave him. Then the clerk fell heavily upon him, clutching him by the throat with feeble fingers. The sharp bite of the axe had caused Cuthfert to drop the pistol, and as his lungs panted for release, he fumbled aimlessly for it among the blankets. Then he remembered. He slid a hand up the clerk's belt to the sheath-knife; and they drew very close to each other in that last clinch.

Percy Cuthfert felt his strength leave him. The lower portion of his body was useless. The inert weight of Weatherbee crushed him,— crushed him and pinned him there like a bear under a trap. The cabin became filled with a familiar odor, and he knew the bread to be burning. Yet what did it matter? He would never need it. And there were all of six cupfuls of sugar in the cache,—if he had foreseen this he would not have been so saving the last several days. Would the wind-vane ever move? It might even be veering now. Why not? Had he not seen the sun to-day? He would go and see. No; it was impossible to move. He had not thought the clerk so heavy a man.

How quickly the cabin cooled! The fire must be out. The cold was forcing in. It must be below zero already, and the ice creeping up the inside of the door. He could not see it, but his past experience enabled him to gauge its progress by the cabin's temperature. The lower

hinge must be white ere now. Would the tale
of this ever reach the world? How would his
friends take it? They would read it over their
coffee, most likely, and talk it over at the clubs.
He could see them very clearly. "Poor Old Cuthfert," they murmured; "not such a bad sort of
a chap, after all." He smiled at their eulogies,
and passed on in search of a Turkish bath. It
was the same old crowd upon the streets.
Strange, they did not notice his moosehide moccasins and tattered German socks! He would
take a cab. And after the bath a shave would
not be bad. No; he would eat first. Steak, and
potatoes, and green things,—how fresh it all was!
And what was that? Squares of honey, streaming liquid amber! But why did they bring so
much? Ha! ha! he could never eat it all. Shine!
Why, certainly. He put his foot on the box. The
bootblack looked curiously up at him, and he
remembered his moosehide moccasins and went
away hastily.

Hark! The wind-vane must be surely spin-
ning. No; a mere singing in his ears. That was
all,—a mere singing. The ice must have passed
the latch by now. More likely the upper hinge
was covered. Between the moss-chinked roof-
poles, little points of frost began to appear. How
slowly they grew! No; not so slowly. There was
a new one, and there another. Two—three—four;
they were coming too fast to count. There were
two growing together. And there, a third had
joined them. Why, there were no more spots.
They had run together and formed a sheet.

Well, he would have company. If Gabriel

ever broke the silence of the North, they would stand together, hand in hand, before the great White Throne. And God would judge them, God would judge them!

Then Percy Cuthfert closed his eyes and dropped off to sleep.

EVEN UNTO DEATH

It might have been due to mere coincidence, it might have been because there are undreamed of bonds between the quick and the dead, and it might have been that Bat Morganston felt a blind consciousness of the future when he turned suddenly to Frona Payne and asked, "Even unto death?"

Frona Payne was startled for the moment. Her shallow nature would not permit her to understand the strength of a strong man's love; such things had no place in her fickle standard. Yet she knew men well enough to repress her inclination to smile; so she looked up to him with her serious child's eyes, placing a hand on each brawny shoulder, and answered, "Even unto death, Bat, dear."

And as he crushed her to him, half-doubting, he passionately cried, "If it should happen so, even in death I shall claim you, and no mortal man shall come between!"

"How absurd," she thought as she freed herself and watched him untangling his dogs. And a handsome fellow he was, as he waded among the fierce brutes, pulling here and shoving there,

cuffing right and left and dragging them over
and under the frozen traces till the team stood
clear. Nipped by the intense cold to a tender
pink, his smooth-shaven face told a plain tale
of strength and indomitability. His hair, falling
about his shoulders in thick masses of silky
brown, was probably more responsible for win-
ning the woman's fleeting affections than all the
rest of him put together. Yet when men ran
their eyes up and down his six feet two of
brawn, they declared him a man, from his
beaded moccasins to the crown of his wolf-skin
cap. But then, they were men.

She kissed him once, twice, and yet a third
time, in her shy trusting way; then he broke out
the sled with the gee-pole, "mushed-up" the
dogs as only a dog-driver can, and swung down
the hill to the main river trail. The meridian
sun, shouldering over the snowy summits to the
south, turned the tiny frost particles to scintillating gems, and through this dazzling gossamer
Bat Morganston disappeared on his journey
down the Yukon to Forty Mile. Down there he
was accounted a king, in virtue of the rich dirt
which was his after the dreary years he had
spent in the darkness of the Arctic Circle.
Dawson had no claims upon him. He did not
own a foot of gravel in the district, nor was he
smitten with its inhabitants—the che-cha-quas
that had rushed in like jackals and spoiled the
good old times when men were men and every
man a brother. In fact, the only reason for his
presence, and a most unstable one at that, was
Frona. He had harnessed his dogs and run up

on the ice to renew the pledges of the previous summer, and to plead for an early date. Well, they were to be married in June, and he was returning to the management of his mines with a light heart. June!—the clean-up promised to be rich; he would sell out; and then, the States, Paris, the world! Of course he doubted—most men do when they leave a pretty woman behind—; but ere he had reached Forty Mile he no longer mistrusted, and by the time he froze his lungs on a moose-hunt and died a month later, he had attained a state of blissful optimism.

Frona waved him good-bye, and also with a light heart turned back to her father's cabin; but then, she had no doubts at all. They were to be married in June. That was all settled. And it was no unpleasant prospect. To tell the truth, she thought she would rather like it. Men thought a great deal of him, and it was a match not to be ashamed of. Besides, he was rich. People who should know said he could at any time clean up half a million, and if his American Creek interests turned out anywhere near as reported, he would be a second MacDonald. Now this meant a great deal, for MacDonald was the richest miner in the North, and the most conservative guessers varied by several millions in the appraisement of his wealth.

Now be it known that the sin Frona Payne committed was a sin of deed, not fact. There were no mail-teams between Forty Mile and Dawson and as Bat Morganston's mines were still a hundred miles into the frozen wilderness from Forty Mile, no news of his death came up the river. And since he had agreed to write only on the highly improbable contingency of a stray traveler passing his diggings, she thought nothing of his silence. To all intents, so far as she was concerned, he was alive. So the sin she committed was of a verity a sin of deed.

By no method may a woman's soul be analyzed, by no scales may a woman's motive be weighed; so no reason can be given for Frona Payne giving her heart and hand to Jack Crelin within three months of her farewell to Bat Morganston. True, Jack Crelin was a Circle City king, possessed of some of the choicest Birch Creek claims; but the men who had made the country did not rate him highly, and his only admirers were to be found among the sycophantic tenderfeet who generously helped him scatter his yellow dust. Perhaps it was the way he had about him, and perhaps it was the impulsive affinity of two shallow souls; but be it what it may, they agreed to marry each other in June, and to journey on down to Circle City and set up housekeeping after the primitive manner of the Northland.

The Yukon broke early, and soon after that important event the river steamer *Cassiar*, captained by her brother, was scheduled to sail. The *Cassiar* had the mingled honor and misfortune to be both the treasure ship and the hospital ship of the year. In her strong boxes she carried five millions of gold, in her staterooms ten score of crippled and diseased. And there were also Lower Country traders and kings, returning from their winter labors or pleasures at

Dawson. Among these—a little anticipation of the event—were listed Mr. and Mrs. Jack Crelin. But when the sick and heart-weary lifted their voices to heaven at the cruel delay, and the gold-shippers waxed clamorous, the *Cassiar* was forced to sail before her time, and Mr. and Mrs. Jack Crelin were yet man and maid.

"Never mind, Frona," her brother said; "come aboard and I'll take charge of you. Father Mahan takes passage at Forty Mile, and you'll be snugly one before we say good-bye at Circle City."

Plimsol marks, boiler inspectors, and protesting boards of underwriters, not yet having penetrated the dismal dominions of the North, the *Cassiar* cast off her lines, with passengers, freight and chattels packed like badly assorted sardines. Wolf-dogs, whose work began and ceased with the snow, and who grew high-stomached with summer idleness, rioted over the steamer from stem to stern or killed each other on the slightest provocation. Stalwart Stick Indians of the Upper River regions lightened their heavy money pouches in brave endeavors to best the white man at his games of chance, or outraged their vitals with the whisky he sold at thirty dollars the bottle. There were squat Mongolian featured Malemute and Innuit wanderers from the Great Dalta two thousand miles away; not among the whites was the jangle of nationalities less pronounced. The nations of the world had sent their sons to the North, and the tongues they spoke were many. In short, the brother of Frona Payne commanded

a floating Babel, commanded and guided it un-
erringly through an uncharted wilderness upon
the breast of a howling flood—for the mighty
Yukon had raised its sullen voice and roared its
anger from mountain rim to mountain rim. Nine
months of snow was passing between its banks
in as many days, and the journey to the sea was
long.

At Forty Mile more passengers and freight
were crowded aboard. Among the pilgrims was
Father Mahan, and in the baggage was an unpainted pine box, corresponding in size to the
conventional last tenement of man. The rush of
life has little heed for death, so this box was
piled precariously upon a pyramid of freight on
the *Cassiar's* deck. But Bat Morganston, having
lain till the moment of shipment in a comfortable ice-cave, did not care. Nobody cared.
There were no mourners, save a huge wolf-dog,
to whom the taste of his master's lash was still
sweet. He crept aboard unnoticed, and ere the
lines were cast off had taken up his accustomed
vigil on the heap of freight by his master's side.
He was such a vicious brute, and had such a
fearful way of baring his fangs, that the other
canine passengers gave him a wide berth,
choosing to leave him alone with his dead.

The cabins were crowded with the sick, so the
marriage began on the stifling deck. It was near
midnight, but the sun, red-disked and somber,
slanted its oblique rays from just above the
northern sky line. Frona Payne and Jack Crelin
stood side by side. Father Mahan began the
service. From aft came the sound of scuffling

among half a dozen drunken gamblers; but in the main the human cargo had crowded about the center of interest. And also the dogs.

Still, all would have been well had not a Labrador dog sought a coign of vantage among the freight. He had traveled countless journeys, was a veteran of a dozen famines and a thousand fights, and knew not fear. The truculent front of the dog which guarded the pine box interested him. He drew in, his naked fangs shining like jeweled ivory. They closed with snap and snarl, the carelessly piled freight tottering beneath them.

At this moment Father Mahan blessed the two which were now one, and Jack Crelin solemnly added, "Even unto death."

"Even unto death," Frona Payne repeated, and her mind leaped back to the other man who had spoken those words. For the instant she felt genuine sorrow and remorse for what she had done. And at that instant the two dogs shut their jaws in the death-grip, and the long pine box poised on the edge of its pyramid. Her husband jerked her from beneath as it fell, end on. There was a crash and splintering; the cover fell away, and Bat Morganston, on his feet, erect, just as in life, with the sun glinting on his silky brown locks, swept forward.

It happened very quickly. Some say that his lips parted in a fearful smile, that he flung his arms about Frona Payne and held her till they fell together to the deck. This would seem impossible, seeing that the man was dead; but there are those who swear that these things were done. However, Frona Payne shrieked terribly as they drew her from beneath the body of her jilted lover, nor did her shrieking cease till land was made at Circle City.

And Bat Morganston's words were true, for to-day, if one should care to journey over to the hills which lie beyond Circle City, he will see, side by side, a cabin and a grave. In the one dwells Frona Payne; in the other Bat Morganston. They are waiting for each other till their fetters shall fall away and the Trump of Doom breaks the silence of the North.

THE MAN
WITH THE GASH

Jacob Kent had suffered from cupidity all the days of his life. This, in turn, had engendered a chronic distrustfulness, and his mind and character had become so warped that he was a very disagreeable man to deal with. He was also a victim to somnambulic propensities, and very set in his ideas. He had been a weaver of cloth from the cradle, until the fever of Klondike had entered his blood and torn him away from his loom. His cabin stood midway between Sixty Mile Post and the Stuart River; and men who made it a custom to travel the trail to Dawson, likened him to a robber baron, perched in his fortress and exacting toll from the caravans that used his ill-kept roads. Since a certain amount of history was required in the construction of this figure, the less cultured way-farers from Stuart River were prone to describe him after a still more primordial fashion, in which a command of strong adjectives was to be chiefly noted.

This cabin was not his, by the way, having

been built several years previously by a couple of miners who had got out a raft of logs at that point for a grub-stake. They had been most hospitable lads, and, after they abandoned it, travelers who knew the route made it an object to arrive there at nightfall. It was very handy, saving them all the time and toil of pitching camp; and it was an unwritten rule that the last man left a neat pile of firewood for the next comer. Rarely a night passed but from half a dozen to a score of men crowded into its shelter. Jacob Kent noted these things, exercised squatter sovereignty, and moved in. Thenceforth, the weary travelers were mulcted a dollar per head for the privilege of sleeping on the floor, Jacob Kent weighing the dust and never failing to steal the down-weight. Besides, he so contrived that his transient guests chopped his wood for him and carried his water. This was rank piracy, but his victims were an easy-going breed, and while they detested him, they yet permitted him to flourish in his sins.

One afternoon in April he sat by his door,—for all the world like a predatory spider,—marvelling at the heat of the returning sun, and keeping an eye on the trail for prospective flies. The Yukon lay at his feet, a sea of ice, disappearing around two great bends to the north and south, and stretching an honest two miles from bank to bank. Over its rough breast ran the sled-trail, a slender sunken line, eighteen inches wide and two thousand miles in length, with more curses distributed to the linear foot than any other road in or out of all Christendom.

Jacob Kent was feeling particularly good that afternoon. The record had been broken the previous night, and he had sold his hospitality to no less than twenty-eight visitors. True, it had been quite uncomfortable, and four had snored beneath his bunk all night; but then it had added appreciable weight to the sack in which he kept his gold dust. That sack, with its glittering yellow treasure, was at once the chief delight and the chief bane of his existence. Heaven and hell lay within its slender mouth. In the nature of things, there being no privacy to his one-roomed dwelling, he was tortured by a constant fear of theft. It would be very easy for these bearded, desperate-looking strangers to make away with it. Often he dreamed that such was the case, and awoke in the grip of nightmare. A select number of these robbers haunted him through his dreams, and he came to know them quite well, especially the bronzed leader with the gash on his right cheek. This fellow was the most persistent of the lot, and, because of him, he had, in his waking moments, constructed several score of hiding-places in and about the cabin. After a concealment he would breathe freely again, perhaps for several nights, only to collar the Man with the Gash in the very act of unearthing the sack. Then, on awakening in the midst of the usual struggle, he would at once get up and transfer the bag to a new and more ingenious crypt. It was not that he was the direct victim of these phantasms; but he believed in omens and thought-transference, and he deemed these dream-robbers to be the astral projection of real personages who happened at those particular moments, no matter where they were in the flesh, to be harboring designs, in the spirit, upon his wealth. So he continued to bleed the unfortunates who crossed his threshold, and at the same time to add to his trouble with every ounce that went into the sack.

As he sat sunning himself, a thought came to Jacob Kent that brought him to his feet with a jerk. The pleasures of life had culminated in the continual weighing and reweighing of his dust; but a shadow had been thrown upon this pleasant avocation, which he had hitherto failed to brush aside. His gold-scales were quite small; in fact, their maximum was a pound and a half,—eighteen ounces,—while his hoard mounted up to something like three and a third times that. He had never been able to weigh it all at one operation, and hence considered himself to have been shut out from a new and most edifying coign of contemplation. Being denied this, half the pleasure of possession had been lost; nay, he felt that this miserable obstacle actually minimized the fact, as it did the strength, of possession. It was the solution of this problem flashing across his mind that had just brought him to his feet. He searched the trail carefully in either direction. There was nothing in sight, so he went inside.

In a few seconds he had the table cleared-away and the scales set up. On one side he placed the stamped disks to the equivalent of fifteen ounces, and balanced it with dust on the other. Replacing the weights with dust, he then had thirty ounces precisely balanced. These, in turn, he placed together on one side and again balanced with more dust. By this time the gold was exhausted, and he was sweating liberally. He trembled with ecstasy, ravished beyond measure. Nevertheless he dusted the sack thoroughly, to the last least grain, till the balance was overcome and one side of the scales sank to the table. Equilibrium, however, was restored by the addition of a pennyweight and five grains to the opposite side. He stood, head thrown back, transfixed. The sack was empty, but the potentiality of the scales had become immeasurable. Upon them he could weigh any amount, from the tiniest grain to pounds upon pounds. Mammon laid hot fingers on his heart. The sun swung on its westering way till it flashed through the open doorway, full upon the yellow-burdened scales. The precious heaps, like the golden breasts of a bronze Cleopatra, flung back the light in a mellow glow. Time and space were not.

"Gawd blime me! but you 'ave the makin' of several quid there, 'aven't you?"

Jacob Kent wheeled about, at the same time reaching for his double-barrelled shot-gun, which stood handy. But when his eyes lit on the intruder's face, he staggered back dizzily. *It was the face of the Man with the Gash!*

The man looked at him curiously.

"Oh, that's all right," he said, waving his hand deprecatingly. "You needn't think as I'll 'arm you or your blasted dust.

"You're a rum 'un, you are," he added reflectively, as he watched the sweat pouring from off Kent's face and the quavering of his knees.

"W'y don't you pipe up an' say somethin'?" he went on, as the other struggled for breath. "Wot's gone wrong o' your gaff? Anythink the matter?"

"W—w—where'd you get it?" Kent at last managed to articulate, raising a shaking forefinger to the ghastly scar which seamed the other's cheek.

"Shipmate stove me down with a marlin-spike from the main-royal. An' now as you 'ave your figger'ead in trim, wot I want to know is, wot's it to you? That's wot I want to know—wot's it to you? Gawd blime me! do it 'urt you? Ain't it smug enough for the likes o' you? That's wot I want to know!"

"No, no," Kent answered, sinking upon a stool with a sickly grin. "I was just wondering."

"Did you ever see the like?" the other went on truculently.

"No."

"Ain't it a beute?"

"Yes." Kent nodded his head approvingly, intent on humoring this strange visitor, but wholly unprepared for the outburst which was to follow his effort to be agreeable.

"You blasted, bloomin', burgoo-eatin' son-of-a-sea-swab! Wot do you mean, a sayin' the most onsightly thing Gawd Almighty ever put on the face o' man is a beute? Wot do you mean, you—"

And thereat this fiery son of the sea broke off into a string of Oriental profanity, mingling gods and devils, lineages and men, metaphors and monsters, with so savage a virility that Jacob Kent was paralyzed. He shrank back, his arms lifted as though to ward off physical violence. So utterly unnerved was he that the other paused in the mid-swing of a gorgeous peroration and burst into thunderous laughter.

"The sun's knocked the bottom out o' the trail," said the Man with the Gash, between departing paroxysms of mirth. "An' I only 'ope as you'll appreciate the hoppertunity of consortin' with a man o' my mug. Get steam up in that fire-box o' your'n. I'm goin' to unrig the dogs an' grub 'em. An' don't be shy o' the wood, my lad; there's plenty more where that come from, and it's you've got the time to sling an axe. An' tote up a bucket o' water while you're about it. Lively! or I'll run you down, so 'elp me!"

Such a thing was unheard of. Jacob Kent was making the fire, chopping wood, packing water—doing menial tasks for a guest! When Jim Cardegee left Dawson, it was with his head filled with the iniquities of this roadside Shylock; and all along the trail his numerous victims had added to the sum of his crimes. Now, Jim Cardegee, with the sailor's love for a sailor's joke, had determined, when he pulled into the cabin, to bring its inmate down a peg or so. That he had succeeded beyond expectation he could not help but remark, though he was in the dark as to the part the gash on his cheek had played in it. But while he could not understand, he saw the terror it created, and resolved to ex-

ploit it as remorselessly as would any modern
trader a choice bit of merchandise.

"Strike me blind, but you're a 'ustler," he said
admiringly, his head cocked to one side, as his
host bustled about. "You never 'ort to 'ave gone
Klondiking. It's the keeper of a pub' you was
laid out for. An' it's often as I 'ave 'eard the lads
up an' down the river speak o' you, but I 'adn't
no idea you was so jolly nice."

Jacob Kent experienced a tremendous yearning to try his shotgun on him, but the fascina-
tion of the gash was too potent. This was the
real Man with the Gash, the man who had so often robbed him in the spirit. This, then, was the
embodied entity of the being whose astral form
had been projected into his dreams, the man
who had so frequently harbored designs against
his hoard; hence—there could be no other conclusion—this Man with the Gash had now come
in the flesh to dispossess him. And that gash! He
could no more keep his eyes from it than stop
the beating of his heart. Try as he would, they
wandered back to that one point as inevitably
as the needle to the pole.

"Do it 'urt you?" Jim Cardegee thundered
suddenly, looking up from the spreading of his
blankets and encountering the rapt gaze of the
other. "It strikes me as 'ow it 'ud be the proper
thing for you to draw your jib, douse the glim,
an' turn in, seein' as 'ow it worrits you. Jes' lay
to that, you swab, or so 'elp me I'll take a pull
on your peak-purchases!"

Kent was so nervous that it took three puffs to
blow out the slush-lamp, and he crawled into

his blankets without even removing his moccasins. The sailor was soon snoring lustily from his hard bed on the floor, but Kent lay staring up into the blackness, one hand on the shotgun, resolved not to close his eyes the whole night. He had not had an opportunity to secrete his five pounds of gold, and it lay in the ammunition box at the head of his bunk. But, try as he would, he at last dozed off with the weight of his dust heavy on his soul. Had he not inadvertently fallen asleep with his mind in such condition, the somnambulic demon would not have been invoked, nor would Jim Cardegee have gone mining next day with a dish-pan.

The fire fought a losing battle, and at last died away, while the frost penetrated the mossy chinks between the logs and chilled the inner atmosphere. The dogs outside ceased their howling, and, curled up in the snow, dreamed of salmon-stocked heavens where dog-drivers and kindred task-masters were not. Within, the sailor lay like a log, while his host tossed restlessly about, the victim of strange fantasies. As midnight drew near he suddenly threw off the blankets and got up. It was remarkable that he could do what he then did without ever striking a light. Perhaps it was because of the darkness that he kept his eyes shut, and perhaps it was for fear he would see the terrible gash on the cheek of his visitor; but, be this as it may, it is a fact that, unseeing, he opened his ammunition box, put a heavy charge into the muzzle of the shotgun without spilling a particle, rammed it down with double wads, and then put everything away and got back into bed.

Just as daylight laid its steel-gray fingers on the parchment window, Jacob Kent awoke. Turning on his elbow, he raised the lid and peered into the ammunition box. Whatever he saw, or whatever he did not see, exercised a very peculiar effect upon him, considering his neurotic temperament. He glanced at the sleeping man on the floor, let the lid down gently, and rolled over on his back. It was an unwonted calm that rested on his face. Not a muscle quivered. There was not the least sign of excitement or perturbation. He lay there a long while, thinking, and when he got up and began to move about, it was in a cool, collected manner, without noise and without hurry.

It happened that a heavy wooden peg had been driven into the ridge-pole just above Jim Cardegee's head. Jacob Kent, working softly, ran a piece of half-inch manila over it, bringing both ends to the ground. One end he tied about his waist, and in the other he rove a running noose. Then he cocked his shotgun and laid it within reach, by the side of numerous moosehide thongs. By an effort of will he bore the sight of the scar, slipped the noose over the sleeper's head, and drew it taut by throwing back on his weight, at the same time seizing the gun and bringing it to bear.

Jim Cardegee awoke, choking, bewildered, staring down the twin wells of steel.

"Where is it?" Kent asked, at the same time slacking on the rope.

"You blasted—ugh—"

Kent merely threw back his weight, shutting off the other's wind.

"Bloomin'—Bur—ugh—"

"Where is it?" Kent repeated.

"Wot?" Cardegee asked, as soon as he had caught his breath.

"The gold-dust."

"Wot gold-dust?" the perplexed sailor demanded.

"You know well enough,—mine."

"Ain't seen nothink of it. Wot do ye take me for? A safe-deposit? Wot 'ave I got to do with it, any'ow?"

"Mebbe you know, and mebbe you don't know, but anyway, I'm going to stop your breath till you do know. And if you lift a hand, I'll blow your head off!"

"Vast heavin'!" Cardegee roared, as the rope tightened.

Kent eased away a moment, and the sailor, wriggling his neck as though from the pressure, managed to loosen the noose a bit and work it up so the point of contact was just under the chin.

"Well?" Kent questioned, expecting the disclosure.

But Cardegee grinned. "Go ahead with your 'angin', you bloomin' old pot-wolloper!"

Then, as the sailor had anticipated, the tragedy became a farce. Cardegee being the heavier of the two, Kent, throwing his body backward and down, could not lift him clear of the ground. Strain and strive to the uttermost, the sailor's feet still stuck to the floor and sustained a part of his weight. The remaining portion was supported by the point of contact just under his chin. Failing to swing him clear, Kent clung on, resolved to slowly throttle him or force him to tell what he had done with the hoard. But the Man with the Gash would not throttle. Five, ten, fifteen minutes passed, and at the end of that time, in despair, Kent let his prisoner down.

"Well," he remarked, wiping away the sweat, "if you won't hang you'll shoot. Some men wasn't born to be hanged, anyway."

"An' it's a pretty mess as you'll make o' this 'ere cabin floor." Cardegee was fighting for time. "Now, look 'ere, I'll tell you wot we do; we'll lay our 'eads 'longside an' reason together. You've lost some dust. You say as 'ow I know, an' I say as 'ow I don't. Let's get a hobservation an' shape a course—"

"Vast heavin'!" Kent dashed in, maliciously imitating the other's enunciation. "I'm going to shape all the courses of this shebang, and you observe; and if you do anything more, I'll bore you as sure as Moses!"

"For the sake of my mother—"

"Whom God have mercy upon if she loves you. Ah! Would you?" He frustrated a hostile move on the part of the other by pressing the cold muzzle against his forehead. "Lay quiet, now! If you lift as much as a hair, you'll get it."

It was rather an awkward task, with the trigger of the gun always within pulling distance of the finger; but Kent was a weaver, and in a few minutes had the sailor tied hand and foot. Then he dragged him without and laid him by the side of the cabin, where he could overlook the river and watch the sun climb to the meridian. "Now I'll give you till noon, and then—"

"Wot?"

"You'll be hitting the brimstone trail. But if you speak up, I'll keep you till the next bunch of mounted police come by."

"Well, Gawd blime me, if this ain't a go! 'Ere I be, innercent as a lamb, an' 'ere you be, lost all o' your top 'amper an' out o' your reckonin', run me foul an' goin' to rake me into 'ell-fire. You bloomin' old pirut! You—"

Jim Cardegee loosed the strings of his profanity and fairly outdid himself. Jacob Kent brought out a stool that he might enjoy it in comfort. Having exhausted all the possible combinations of his vocabulary, the sailor quieted down to hard thinking, his eyes constantly gauging the progress of the sun, which tore up the eastern slope of the heavens with unseemly haste. His dogs, surprised that they had not long since been put to harness, crowded around him. His helplessness appealed to the brutes. They felt that something was wrong, though they knew not what, and they crowded about, howling their mournful sympathy.

"Chook! Mush-on! you Siwashes!" he cried, attempting, in a vermicular way, to kick at them, and discovering himself to be tottering on the edge of declivity. As soon as the animals had scattered, he devoted himself to the significance of that declivity which he felt to be there

but could not see. Nor was he long in arriving at
a correct conclusion. In the nature of things, he
figured, man is lazy. He does no more than he
has to. When he builds a cabin he must put dirt
on the roof. From these premises it was logical
that he should carry that dirt no further than
was absolutely necessary. Therefore, he lay
upon the edge of the hole from which the dirt
had been taken to roof Jacob Kent's cabin. This
knowledge, properly utilized, might prolong
things, he thought; and he then turned his attention to the moose-hide thongs which bound
him. His hands were tied behind him, and
pressing against the snow, they were wet with
the contact. This moistening of the raw-hide he
knew would tend to make it stretch, and, without apparent effort, he endeavored to stretch it
more and more.

He watched the trail hungrily, and when in
the direction of Sixty Mile a dark speck appeared for a moment against the white background of an icejam, he cast an anxious eye at
the sun. It had climbed nearly to the zenith.
Now and again he caught the black speck clearing the hills of ice and sinking into the intervening hollows; but he dared not permit himself
more than the most cursory glances for fear of
rousing his enemy's suspicion. Once, when
Jacob Kent rose to his feet and searched the
trail with care, Cardegee was frightened, but
the dog-sled had struck a piece of trail running
parallel with a jam, and remained out of sight
till the danger was past.

"I'll see you 'ung for this," Cardegee

threatened, attempting to draw the other's attention. "An' you'll rot in 'ell, jes' you see if you don't.

"I say," he cried, after another pause; "d' ye b'lieve in ghosts?" Kent's sudden start made him sure of his ground, and he went on: "Now a ghost 'as the right to 'aunt a man wot don't do wot he says; and you can't shuffle me off till eight bells—wot I mean is twelve o'clock—can you? 'Cos if you do, it'll 'appen as 'ow I'll 'aunt you. D'ye 'ear? A minute, a second too quick, an' I'll 'aunt you, so 'elp me, I will!"

Jacob Kent looked dubious, but declined to talk. "'Ow's your chronometer? Wot's your longitude? 'Ow do you know as your time's corect?" Cardegee persisted, vainly hoping to beat his executioner out of a few minutes. "Is it Barrack's time you 'ave, or is it the Company time? 'Cos if you do it before the stroke o' the bell, I'll not rest. I give you fair warnin' I'll come back. An' if you 'aven't the time, 'ow will you know? That's wot I want—'ow will you tell?"

"I'll send you off all right;" Kent replied.

"Got a sun-dial here."

"No good. Thirty-two degrees variation o' the needle."

"Stakes are all set."

"'Ow did you set 'em? Compass?"

"No; lined them up with the North Star."

"Sure?"

"Sure."

Cardegee groaned, then stole a glance at the trail. The sled was just clearing a rise, barely a mile away, and the dogs were in full lope, running lightly.

"'Ow close is the shadows to the line?"

Kent walked to the primitive timepiece and studied it. "Three inches," he announced, after a careful survey.

"Say, jes' sing out 'eight bells' afore you pull the gun, will you?"

Kent agreed, and they lapsed into silence. The thongs about Cardegee's wrists were slowly stretching, and he had begun to work them over his hands.

"Say, 'ow close is the shadows?"

"One inch."

The sailor wriggled slightly to assure himself that he would topple over at the right moment, and slipped the first turn over his hands.

"'Ow close?"

"Half an inch." Just then Kent heard the jarring churn of the runners and turned his eyes to the trail. The driver was lying flat on the sled and the dogs swinging down the straight stretch to the cabin. Kent whirled back, bringing his rifle to shoulder.

"It ain't eight bells yet!" Cardegee expostulated. "I'll 'aunt you, sure!"

Jacob Kent faltered. He was standing by the sun-dial, perhaps ten paces from his victim. The man on the sled must have seen that something unusual was taking place, for he had risen to his knees, his whip singing viciously among the dogs.

The shadows swept into line. Kent looked along the sights.

"Make ready!" he commanded solemnly. "Eight b—"

But just a fraction of a second too soon, Cardegee rolled backward into the hole. Kent held his fire and ran to the edge. Bang! The gun exploded full in the sailor's face as he rose to his feet. But no smoke came from the muzzle; instead, a sheet of flame burst from the side of the barrel near its butt, and Jacob Kent went down. The dogs dashed up the bank, dragging the sled over his body, and the driver sprang off as Jim Cardegee freed his hands and drew himself from the hole.

"Jim!" The new-comer recognized him.

"What's the matter?"

"Wot's the matter? Oh, nothink at all. It jest 'appens as I do little things like this for my 'ealth. Wot's the matter, you bloomin' idjit? Wot's the matter, eh' Cast me loose or I'll show you wot! 'Urry up, or I'll 'olystone the decks with you!"

"Huh!" he added, as the other went to work with his sheath-knife. "Wot's the matter? I want to know. Jes' tell me that, will you, wot's the matter? Hey?"

Kent was quite dead when they rolled him over. The gun, an old-fashioned, heavy-weighted muzzle-loader, lay near him. Steel and wood had parted company. Near the butt of the right-hand barrel, with lips pressed outward, gaped a fissure several inches in length. The sailor picked it up, curiously. A glittering stream of yellow dust ran out through the crack. The facts of the case dawned upon Jim Cardegee.

"Strike me standin'!" he roared; " 'ere's a go!
'Ere's 'is bloomin' dust! Gawd blime me, an'
you, too, Charley, if you don't run an' get the
dish-pan!"

THE
ONE THOUSAND DOZEN

David Rasmunsen was a hustler, and, like many a greater man, a man of the one idea. Wherefore, when the clarion call of the North rang on his ear, he conceived an adventure in eggs and bent all his energy to its achievement. He figured briefly and to the point, and the adventure became iridescent-hued, splendid. That eggs would sell at Dawson for five dollars a dozen was a safe working premise. Whence it was incontrovertible that one thousand dozen would bring, in the Golden Metropolis, five thousand dollars.

On the other hand, expense was to be considered, and he considered it well, for he was a careful man, keenly practical, with a hard head and a heart that imagination never warmed. At fifteen cents a dozen, the initial cost of his thousand dozen would be one hundred and fifty dollars, a mere bagatelle in face of the enormous profit. And suppose, just suppose, to be wildly extravagant for once, that transportation for himself and eggs should run up eight hundred and fifty more; he would still have four thousand clear cash and clean when the last egg was disposed of and the last dust had rippled into his sack.

"You see, Alma,"—he figured it over with his wife, the cosy dining room submerged in a sea of maps, government surveys, guidebooks, and Alaskan itineraries,—"you see, expenses don't really begin till you make Dyea—fifty dollars'll cover it with a first-class passage thrown in. Now from Dyea to Lake Linderman, Indian packers take your goods over for twelve cents a pound, twelve dollars a hundred, or one hundred and twenty dollars a thousand. Say I have fifteen hundred pounds, it'll cost one hundred and eighty dollars—call it two hundred and be safe. I am creditably informed by a Klondiker just come out that I can buy a boat for three hundred. But the same man says I'm sure to get a couple of passengers for one hundred and fifty each, which will give me the boat for nothing, and, further, they can help me manage it. And . . . that's all; I put my eggs ashore from the boat at Dawson. Now let me see how much is that?"

"Fifty dollars from San Francisco to Dyea, two hundred from Dyea to Linderman, passengers pay for the boat—two hundred and fifty all told," she summed up swiftly.

"And a hundred for my clothes and personal outfit," he went on happily; "that leaves a margin of five hundred for emergencies. And what possible emergencies can arise?"

Alma shrugged her shoulders and elevated

her brows. If that vast Northland was capable of swallowing up a man and a thousand dozen eggs, surely there was room and to spare for whatever else he might happen to possess. So she thought, but she said nothing. She knew David Rasmunsen too well to say anything.

"Doubling the time because of chance delays, I should make the trip in two months. Think of it, Alma! Four thousand in two months! Beats the paltry hundred a month I'm getting now. Why, we'll build further out where we'll have more space, gas in every room, and a view, and the rent of the cottage'll pay more space, gas in every room, and a view, and the rent of the cottage'll pay more space, gas in every room, and a view, and the rent of the cottage'll pay taxes, insurance, and water, and leave something over. And then there's always the chance of my striking it and coming out a millionaire. Now tell me, Alma, don't you think I'm very moderate?"

And Alma could hardly think otherwise. Besides, had not her own cousin,—though a remote and distant one to be sure, the black sheep, the harum-scarum, the ne'er-do-well,— had not he come down out of that weird North country with a hundred thousand in yellow dust, to say nothing of a half-ownership in the hole from which it came?

David Rasmunsen's grocer was surprised when he found him weighing eggs in the scales at the end of the counter, and Rasmunsen himself was more surprised when he found that a dozen eggs weighed a pound and a half—fifteen hundred pounds for his thousand dozen! There

would be no weight left for his clothes, blankets,
and cooking utensils, to say nothing of the grub
he must necessarily consume by the way. His
calculations were all thrown out, and he was
just proceeding to recast them when he hit upon
the idea of weighing small eggs. "For whether
they be large or small, a dozen eggs is a dozen
eggs," he observed sagely to himself; and a
dozen small ones he found to weigh but a
pound and a quarter. Thereat the city of San
Francisco was overrun by anxious-eyed emis-
saries, and commission houses and dairy associ-
ations were startled by a sudden demand for
eggs running not more than twenty ounces to
the dozen.

Rasmunsen mortgaged the little cottage for a
thousand dollars, arranged for his wife to make
a prolonged stay among her own people, threw
up his job, and started North. To keep within
his schedule he compromised on a second-class
passage, which, because of the rush, was worse
than steerage; and in the late summer, a pale
and wabbly man, he disembarked with his eggs
on the Dyea beach. But it did not take him long
to recover his land legs and appetite. His first
interview   with   the   Chilkoot   packers
straightened him up and stiffened his backbone.
Forty cents a pound they demanded for the
twenty-eight-mile portage, and while he caught
hin breath and swallowed, the price went
up to forty-three. Fifteen husky Indians put
the straps on his packs at forty-five, but took
them off at an offer of forty-seven from a
Skaguay Croesus in dirty shirt and ragged over-

alls who had lost his horses on the White Pass Trail and was now making a last desperate drive at the country by way of Chilkoot.

But Rasmunsen was clean grit, and at fifty cents found takers, who, two days later, set his eggs down intact at Linderman. But fifty cents a pound is a thousand dollars a ton, and his fifteen hundred pounds had exhausted his emergency fund and left him stranded at the Tantalus point where each day he saw the fresh-whip-sawed boats departing for Dawson. Further, a great anxiety brooded over the camp where the boats were built. Men worked frantically, early and late, at the height of their endurance, calking, nailing, and pitching in a frenzy of haste for which adequate explanation was not far to seek. Each day the snow-line crept farther down the bleak, rock-shouldered peaks, and gale followed gale, with sleet and slush and snow, and in the eddies and quiet places young ice formed and thickened through the fleeting hours. And each morn, toil-stiffened men turned wan faces across the lake to see if the freeze-up had come. For the freeze-up heralded the death of their hope—the hope that they would be floating down the swift river ere navigation closed on the chain of lakes.

To harrow Rasmunsen's soul further, he discovered three competitors in the egg business. It was true that one, a little German, had gone broke and was himself forlornly back-tripping the last pack of the portage; but the other two had boats nearly completed and were daily supplicating the god of merchants and traders to

stay the iron hand of winter for just another
day. But the iron hand closed down over the
land. Men were being frozen in the blizzard,
which swept Chilkoot, and Rasmunsen frosted
his toes ere he was aware. He found a chance to
go passenger with his freight in a boat just shoving off through the rubble, but two hundred,
hard cash, was required, and he had no money.

"Ay tank you yust wait one leedle w'ile," said
the Swedish boat-builder, who had struck his
Klondike right there and was wise enough to
know it—"one leedle w'ile and I make you a tam
fine skiff boat, sure Pete."

With this unpledged word to go on, Rasmunsen hit the back trail to Crater Lake, where he
fell in with two press correspondents whose
tangled baggage was strewn from Stone House,
over across the Pass, and as far as Happy Camp.

"Yes," he said with consequence. "I've a thousand dozen eggs at Linderman, and my boat's
just about got the last seam calked. Consider
myself in luck to get it. Boats are at a premium,
you know, and none to be had."

Whereupon and almost with bodily violence
the correspondents clamored to go with him,
fluttered greenbacks before his eyes, and spilled
yellow twenties from hand to hand. He could
not hear of it, but they overpersuaded him, and
he reluctantly consented to take them at three
hundred apiece. Also they pressed upon him the
passage money in advance. And while they
wrote to their respective journals concerning the
good Samaritan with the thousand dozen eggs,

the good Samaritan was hurrying back to the Swede at Linderman.

"Here, you! Gimme that boat!" was his salutation, his hand jingling the correspondents' gold pieces and his eyes hungrily bent upon the finished craft.

The Swede regarded him stolidly and shook his head.

"How much is the other fellow paying? Three hundred? Well, here's four. Take it."

He tried to press it upon him, but the man backed away.

"Ay tank not. Ay say him get der skiff boat. You yust wait—"

"Here's six hundred. Last call. Take it or leave it. Tell'm it's a mistake."

The Swede wavered. "Ay tank yes," he finally said, and the last Rasmunsen saw of him his vocabulary was going to wreck in a vain effort to explain the mistake to the other fellows.

The German slipped and broke his ankle on the steep hogback above Deep Lake, sold out his stock for a dollar a dozen, and with the proceeds hired Indian packers to carry him back to Dyea. But on the morning Rasmunsen shoved off with his correspondents, his two rivals followed suit.

"How many you got?" one of them, a lean little New Englander, called out.

"One thousand dozen," Rasmunsen answered proudly.

"Huh! I'll go you even stakes I beat you in with my eight hundred."

The correspondents offered to lend him the

money; but Rasmunsen declined, and the Yankee closed with the remaining rival, a brawny son of the sea and sailor of ships and things, who promised to show them all a wrinkle or two when it came to cracking on. And crack on he did, with a large tarpaulin squaresail which pressed the bow half under at every jump. He was the first to run out of Linderman, but, disdaining the portage, piled his loaded boat on the rocks in the boiling rapids. Rasmunsen and the Yankee, who likewise had two passengers, portaged across on their backs and then lined their empty boats down through the bad water to Bennett.

Bennett was a twenty-five-mile lake, narrow and deep, a funnel between the mountains through which storms ever romped. Rasmunsen camped on the sand-pit at its head, where were many men and boats bound north in the teeth of the Arctic winter. He awoke in the morning to find a piping gale from the south, which caught the chill from the whited peaks and glacial valleys and blew as cold as north wind ever blew. But it was fair, and he also found the Yankee staggering past the first bold headland with all sail set Boat after boat was getting under way, and the correspondents fell to with enthusiasm.

"We'll catch him before Cariboo Crossing," they assured Rasmunsen, as they ran up the sail and the *Alma* took the first icy spray over her bow.

Now Rasmunsen all his life had been prone to cowardice on water, but he clung to the kicking steering-oar with set face and determined jaw. His thousand dozen were there in the boat before his eyes, safely secured beneath the correspondents' baggage, and somehow, before his eyes, were the little cottage and the mortgage for a thousand dollars.

It was bitter cold. Now and again he hauled in the steering-sweep and put out a fresh one while his passengers chopped the ice from the blade. Wherever the spray struck, it turned instantly to frost, and the dipping boom of the spritsail was quickly fringed with icicles. The *Alma* strained and hammered through the big seas till the seams and butts began to spread, but in lieu of bailing the correspondents chopped ice and flung it overboard. There was no let-up. The mad race with winter was on, and the boats tore along in a desperate string.

"W-w-we can't stop to save our souls!" one of the correspondents chattered, from cold, not fright.

"That's right! Keep her down the middle, old man!" the other encouraged.

Rasmunsen replied with an idiotic grin. The iron-bound shores were in a lather of foam, and even down the middle the only hope was to keep running away from the big seas. To lower sail was to be overtaken and swamped. Time and again they passed boats pounding among the rocks, and once they saw one on the edge of the breakers about to strike. A little craft behind them, with two men, jibed over and turned bottom up.

"W-w-watch out, old man!" cried he of the chattering teeth

Rasmunsen grinned and tightened his aching grip on the sweep. Scores of times had the send of the sea caught the big square stern of the *Alma* and thrown her off from dead before it till the after leach of the spritsail fluttered hollowly, and each time, and only with all his strength, had he forced her back. His grin by then had become fixed, and it disturbed the correspondents to look at him.

They roared down past an isolated rock a hundred yards from shore. From its wave-drenched top a man shrieked wildly, for the instant cutting the storm with his voice. But the next instant the *Alma* was by, and the rock growing a black speck in the troubled froth.

"That settles the Yankee! Where's the sailor?" shouted one of his passengers.

Rasmunsen shot a glance over his shoulder at a black squaresail. He had seen it leap up out of the gray to windward, and for an hour, off and on, had been watching it grow. The sailor had evidently repaired damages and was making up for lost time.

"Look at him come!"

Both passengers stopped chopping ice to watch. Twenty miles of Bennett were behind them—room and to spare for the sea to toss up its mountains toward the sky. Sinking and soaring like a storm god, the sailor drove by them. The huge sail seemed to grip the boat from the crests of the waves, to tear it bodily out of the water, and fling it crashing and smothering down into the yawning troughs.

"The sea'll never catch him!"

"But he'll r-r-run her nose under!"

Even as they spoke, the black tarpaulin swooped from sight behind a big comber. The next wave rolled over the spot, and the next, but the boat did not reappear. The *Alma* rushed by the place. A little riffraff of oars and boxes was seen. An arm thrust up and a shaggy head broke surface a score of yards away.

For a time there was silence. As the end of the lake came in sight, the waves began to leap aboard with such steady recurrence that the correspondents no longer chopped ice but flung the water out with buckets. Even this would not do, and, after a shouted conference with Rasmunsen, they attacked the baggage. Flour, bacon, beans, blankets, cooking stove, ropes, odds and ends, everything they could get hands on, flew overboard. The boat acknowledged it at once, taking less water and rising more buoyantly.

"That'll do!" Rasmunsen called sternly, as they applied themselves to the top layer of eggs.

"The h-hell it will!" answered the shivering one, savagely. With the exception of their notes, films, and cameras, they had sacrificed their outfit. He bent over, laid hold of an egg-box, and began to worry it out from under the lashing.

"Drop it! Drop it, I say!"

Rasmunsen had managed to draw his revolver, and with the crook of his arm over the sweep head was taking aim. The correspondent stood up on the thwart, balancing back and forth, his face twisted with menace and speechless anger.

"My God!"

So cried his brother correspondent, hurling himself, face downward, into the bottom of the boat. The *Alma*, under the divided attention of Rasmunsen, had been caught by a great mass of water and whirled around. The after leach hollowed, the sail emptied and jibed, and the boom, sweeping with terrific force across the boat, carried the angry correspondent overboard with a broken back. Mast and sail had gone over the side as well. A drenching sea followed, as the boat lost headway, and Rasmunsen sprang to the bailing bucket.

Several boats hurtled past them in the next half-hour,—small boats, boats of their own size, boats afraid, unable to do aught but run madly on Then a ten-ton barge, at imminent risk of destruction, lowered sail to windward and lumbered down upon them.

"Keep off! Keep off!" Rasmunsen screamed.

But his low gunwale ground against the heavy craft, and the remaining correspondent clambered aboard. Rasmunsen was over the eggs like a cat and in the bow of the *Alma*, striving with numb fingers to bend the hauling-lines together.

"Come on!" a red-whiskered man yelled at him.

"I've a thousand dozen eggs here," he shouted back. "Gimme a tow! I'll pay you!"

"Come on!" they howled in chorus.

A big whitecap broke just beyond, washing over the barge and leaving the *Alma* half swamped. The men cast off, cursing him as they ran up their sail. Rasmunsen cursed back and fell to bailing. The mast and sail, like a sea anchor, still fast by the halyards, held the boat head on to wind and sea and gave him a chance to fight the water out.

Three hours later, numbed, exhausted, blathering like a lunatic, but still bailing, he went ashore on an ice-strewn beach near Cariboo Crossing. Two men, a government courier and a half-breed voyageur, dragged him out of the surf, saved his cargo, and beached the *Alma*. They were paddling out of the country in a Peterborough, and gave him shelter for the night in their storm-bound camp. Next morning they departed, but he elected to stay by his eggs. And thereafter the name and fame of the man with the thousand dozen eggs began to spread through the land. Gold-seekers who made in before the freeze-up carried the news of his coming. Grizzled old-timers of Forty Mile and Circle City, sour doughs with leathern jaws and bean-calloused stomachs, called up dream memories of chickens and green things at mention of his name Dyea and Skaguay took an interest in his being, and questioned his progress from every man who came over the passes, while Dawson—golden, omeletless Dawson—fretted and worried, and waylaid every chance arrival for word of him.

But of this, Rasmunsen knew nothing. The

day after the wreck he patched up the *Alma* and pulled out. A cruel east wind blew in his teeth from Tagish, but he got the oars over the side and bucked manfully into it, though half the time he was drifting backward and chopping ice from the blades. According to the custom of the country, he was driven ashore at Windy Arm; three times on Tagish saw him swamped and beached; and Lake Marsh held him at the freeze-up. The *Alma* was crushed in the jamming of the floes, but the eggs were intact. These he backtripped two miles across the ice to the shore, where he built a cache, which stood for years after and was pointed out by men who knew.

Half a thousand frozen miles stretched between him and Dawson, and the waterway was closed. But Rasmunsen, with a peculiar tense look in his face, struck back up the lakes on foot. What he suffered on that lone trip, with naught but a single blanket, an axe, and a handful of beans, is not given to ordinary mortals to know. Only the Arctic adventurer may understand. Suffice that he was caught in a blizzard on Chilkoot and left two of his toes with the surgeon at Sheep Camp. Yet he stood on his feet and washed dishes in the scullery of the *Pawona* to the Puget Sound, and from there passed coal on a P.S. boat to San Francisco.

It was a haggard, unkempt man who limped across the shining office floor to raise a second mortgage from the bank people. His hollow cheeks betrayed themselves through the scraggly beard, and his eyes seemed to have retired into deep caverns where they burned with cold fires. His hands were grained from exposure and hard work, and the nails were rimmed with tight-packed dirt and coal dust. He spoke vaguely of eggs and ice-packs, winds and tides; but when they declined to let him have more than a second thousand, his talk became incoherent, concerning itself chiefly with the price of dogs and dog-food, and such things as snowshoes and moccasins and winter trails. They let him have fifteen hundred, which was more than the cottage warranted, and breathed easier when he scrawled his signature and passed out the door.

Two weeks later he went over Chilkoot with three dog sleds of five dogs each. One team he drove, the two Indians with him driving the other. At Lake Marsh they broke out the cache and loaded up. But there was no trail. He was the first in over the ice, and to him fell the task of packing the snow and hammering away through the rough river jams. Behind him he often observed a camp-fire smoke trickling thinly up through the quiet air, and he wondered why the people did not overtake him. For he was a stranger to the land and did not understand. Nor could he understand his Indians when they tried to explain. This they conceived to be a hardship, but when they balked and refused to break camp of mornings, he drove them to their work at pistol point.

When he slipped through an ice bridge near the White Horse and froze his foot, tender yet and oversensitive from the previous freezing,

the Indians looked for him to lie up. But he
sacrificed a blanket, and, with his foot encased
in an enormous moccasin, big as a water-bucket,
continued to take his regular turn with the front
sled. Here was the cruelest work, and they respected him, though on the side they rapped
their foreheads with their knuckles and signifi-
cantly shook their heads. One night they tried
to run away, but the zip-zip of his bullets in the
snow brought them back, snarling but con-
vinced. Whereupon, being only savage Chilkat
men, they put their heads together to kill him;
but he slept like a cat, and, waking or sleeping,
the chance never came. Often they tried to tell
him the import of the smoke wreath in the rear,
but he could not comprehend and grew suspi-
cious of them. And when they sulked or shirked,
he was quick to let drive at them between the
eyes, and quick to cool their heated souls with
sight of his ready revolver

And so it went—with mutinous men, wild
dogs, and a trail that broke the heart. He fought
the men to stay with him, fought the dogs to
keep them away from the eggs, fought the ice,
the cold, and the pain of his foot, which would
not heal. As fast as the young tissue renewed, it
was bitten and seared by the frost, so that a
running sore developed, into which he could almost shove his fist. In the mornings, when he
first put his weight upon it, his head went dizzy,
and he was near to fainting from the pain; but
later on in the day it usually grew numb, to
recommence when he crawled into his blankets
and tried to sleep. Yet he, who had been a clerk

and sat at a desk all his days, toiled till the Indians were exhausted, and even out-worked the dogs. How hard he worked, how much he suffered, he did not know. Being a man of the one idea, now that the idea had come, it mastered him. In the foreground of his consciousness was Dawson, in the background his thousand dozen eggs, and midway between the two his ego fluttered, striving alway to draw them together to a glittering golden point. This golden point was the five thousand dollars, the consummation of the idea and the point of departure for whatever new idea might present itself. For the rest, he was a mere automaton. He was unaware of other things, seeing them as through a glass darkly, and giving them no thought. The work of his hands he did with machine-like wisdom; likewise the work of his head. So the look on his face grew very tense, till even the Indians were afraid of it, and marvelled at the strange white man who had made them slaves and forced them to toil with such foolishness.

Then came a snap on Lake Le Barge, when the cold of outer space smote the tip of the planet, and the frost ranged sixty and odd degrees below zero. Here, laboring with open mouth that he might breathe more freely, he chilled his lungs, and for the rest of the trip he was troubled with a dry, hacking cough, especially irritable in smoke of camp or under stress of undue exertion. On the Thirty Mile River he found much open water, spanned by precarious ice bridges and fringed with narrow rim ice, tricky and uncertain. The rim ice was impossible to reckon on, and he dared it without reckoning, falling back on his revolver when his drivers demurred. But on the ice bridges, covered with snow though they were, precautions could be taken These they crossed on their snowshoes, with long poles, held crosswise in their hands, to which to cling in case of accident. Once over, the dogs were called to follow. And on such a bridge, where the absence of the centre ice was masked by the snow, one of the Indians met his end. He went through as quickly and neatly as a knife through thin cream, and the current swept him from view down under the stream ice.

That night his mate fled away through the pale moonlight, Rasmunsen futilely puncturing the silence with his revolver—a thing that he handled with more celerity than cleverness. Thirty-six hours later the Indian made a police camp on the Big Salmon.

"Um-um-um funny mans—what you call?—top um head all loose," the interpreter explained to the puzzled captain. "Eh! Yep, clazy, much clazy mans. Eggs, eggs, all a time eggs—savvy? Come bime-by."

It was several days before Rasmunsen arrived, the three sleds lashed together, and all the dogs in a single team. It was awkward, and where the going was bad he was compelled to back-trip it sled by sled, though he managed most of the time, through herculean efforts, to bring all along on the one haul. He did not seem moved when the captain of police told him his man was hitting the high places for Dawson, and was by that time, probably, halfway between Selkirk and Stewart. Nor did he appear interested when informed that the police had broken the trail as far as Pelly; for he had attained to a fatalistic acceptance of all natural dispensations, good or ill. But when they told him that Dawson was in the bitter clutch of famine, he smiled, threw the harness on his dogs, and pulled out.

But it was at his next halt that the mystery of the smoke was explained. With the word at Big Salmon that the trail was broken to Pelly, there was no longer any need for the smoke wreath to linger in his wake; and Rasmunsen, crouching over his lonely fire, saw a motley string of sleds go by. First came the courier and the half-breed who had hauled him out from Bennett; then mail-carriers for Circle City, two sleds of them, and a mixed following of ingoing Klondikers. Dogs and men were fresh and fat, while Rasmunsen and his brutes were jaded and worn down to the skin and bone They of the smoke wreath had travelled one day in three, resting and reserving their strength for the dash to come when broken trail was met with; while each day he had plunged and floundered forward, breaking the spirit of his dogs and robbing them of their mettle.

As for himself, he was unbreakable. They thanked him kindly for his efforts in their behalf, those fat, fresh men,—thanked him kindly, with broad grins and ribald laughter; and now, when he understood, he made no answer. Nor did he cherish silent bitterness. It was im-

material. The idea—the fact behind the idea—
was not changed. Here he was and his thousand
dozen; there was Dawson; the problem was
unaltered.

At the Little Salmon, being short of dog food,
the dogs got into his grub, and from there to
Selkirk he lived on beans—coarse, brown beans,
big beans, grossly nutritive, which griped his
stomach and doubled him up at two-hour intervals. But the Factor at Selkirk had a notice on
the door of the Post to the effect that no steamer
had been up the Yukon for two years, and in
consequence grub was beyond price. He offered
to swap flour, however, at the rate of a cupful
for each egg, but Rasmunsen shook his head
and hit the trail. Below the Post he managed to
buy frozen horse hide for the dogs, the horses
having been slain by the Chilkat cattle men,
and the scraps and offal preserved by the Indians. He tackled the hide himself, but the hair
worked into the bean sores of his mouth, and
was beyond endurance.

Here at Selkirk, he met the forerunners of the
hungry exodus of Dawson, and from there on
they crept over the trail, a dismal throng. "No
grub!" was the song they sang. "No grub, and
had to go." "Everybody holding candles for a
rise in the spring." "Flour dollar'n a half a
pound, and no sellers."

"Eggs?" one of them answered "Dollar
apiece, but they ain't none."

Rasmunsen made a rapid calculation.
"Twelve thousand dollars," he said aloud.

"Hey?" the man asked.

"Nothing," he answered, and *mushed* the dogs along.

When he arrived at Stewart River, seventy miles from Dawson, five of his dogs were gone, and the remainder were falling in the traces. He, also, was in the traces, hauling with what little strength was left in him. Even then he was barely crawling along ten miles a day. His cheek-bones and nose, frost-bitten again and again, were turned bloody-black and hideous. The thumb, which was separated from the fingers by the gee-pole, had likewise been nipped and gave him great pain. The monstrous moccasin still encased his foot, and strange pains were beginning to rack the leg. At Sixty Mile, the last beans, which he had been rationing for some time, were finished; yet he steadfastly refused to touch the eggs. He could not reconcile his mind to the legitimacy of it, and staggered and fell along the way to Indian River. Here a fresh-killed moose and an open-handed old-timer gave him and his dogs new strength, and at Ainslie's, he felt repaid for it all when a stampede, ripe from Dawson in five hours, was sure he could get a dollar and a quarter for every egg he possessed.

He came up the steep bank by the Dawson barracks with fluttering heart and shaking knees. The dogs were so weak that he was forced to rest them, and, waiting, he leaned limply against the gee-pole A man, an eminently decorous-looking man, came sauntering by in a great bearskin coat. He glanced at Rasmunsen curiously, then stopped and ran a speculative eye over the dogs and the three lashed sleds.

"What you got?" he asked.

"Eggs," Rasmunsen answered huskily, hardly able to pitch his voice above a whisper.

"Eggs! Whoopee! Whoopee!" He sprang up into the air, gyrated madly, and finished with half a dozen war steps. "You don't say—all of 'em?"

"All of em?"

"Say, you must be the Egg Man." He walked around and viewed Rasmunsen from the other side. "Come, now, ain't you the Egg Man?"

Rasmunsen didn't know, but supposed he was, and the man sobered down a bit.

"What d'ye expect to get for 'em?" he asked cautiously.

Rasmunsen became audacious. "Dollar'n a half," he said.

"Done!" the man came back promptly. "Gimme a dozen."

"I-I mean a dollar'n a half apiece," Rasmunsen hesitatingly explained.

"Sure. I heard you. Make it two dozen. Here's the dust."

The man pulled out a healthy gold sack the size of a small sausage and knocked it negligently against the gee-pole. Rasmunsen felt a strange trembling in the pit of his stomach, a tickling of the nostrils, and an almost overwhelming desire to sit down and cry. But a curious, wide-eyed crowd was beginning to collect, and man after man was calling out for eggs. He was without scales, but the man with the bearskin coat fetched a pair and obligingly weighed in the dust while Rasmunsen passed out the goods. Soon there was a pushing and shoving and shouldering, and a great clamor. Everybody wanted to buy and to be served first. And as the excitement grew, Rasmunsen cooled down. This would never do. There must be something behind the fact of their buying so eagerly. It would be wiser if he rested first and sized up the market. Perhaps eggs were worth two dollars apiece. Anyway, whenever he wished to sell, he was sure of a dollar and a half. "Stop!" he cried, when a couple of hundred had been sold. "No more now. I'm played out I've got to get a cabin, and then you can come and see me."

A groan went up at this, but the man with the bearskin coat approved. Twenty-four of the frozen eggs went rattling in his capacious pockets and he didn't care whether the rest of the town ate or not. Besides, he could see Rasmunsen was on his last legs.

"There's a cabin right around the second corner from the Monte Carlo," he told him—"the one with the sody-bottle window. It ain't mine, but I've got charge of it. Rents for ten a day and cheap for the money. You move right in, and I'll see you later. Don't forget the sody-bottle window."

"Tra-la-loo!" he called back a moment later. "I'm goin' up the hill to eat eggs and dream of home."

On his way to the cabin, Rasmunsen recollected he was hungry and bought a small supply of provisions at the N. A. T. & T. store—also a beef-steak at the butcher shop and dried salmon for the dogs. He found the cabin without difficulty and left the dogs in harness while he started the fire and got the coffee under way.

"A dollar'n a half apiece—one thousand dozen—eighteen thousand dollars!" He kept muttering it to himself, over and over, as he went about his work

As he flopped the steak into the frying-pan the door opened. He turned. It was the man with the bearskin coat. He seemed to come in with determination, as though bound on some explicit errand, but as he looked at Rasmunsen an expression of perplexity came into his face.

"I say—now I say—" he began, then halted.

Rasmunsen wondered if he wanted the rent.

"I say, damn it, you know, them eggs is bad."

Rasmunsen staggered. He felt as though some one had struck him an astounding blow between the eyes. The walls of the cabin reeled and tilted up. He put out his hand to steady himself and rested it on the stove. The sharp pain and the smell of burning flesh brought him back to himself.

"I see," he said slowly, fumbling in his pocket for the sack. "You want your money back."

"It ain't the money," the man said, "but hain't you got any eggs—good?"

Rasmunsen shook his head. "You'd better take the money."

But the man refused and backed away. "I'll come back," he said, "when you've taken stock, and get what's comin'."

Rasmunsen rolled the chopping-block into the cabin and carried in the eggs. He went about it quite calmly. He took up the hand-axe, and, one by one, chopped the eggs in half. These halves he examined carefully and let fall to the floor. At first, he sampled from the different cases, then deliberately emptied one case at a time. The heap on the floor grew larger. The coffee boiled over and the smoke of the burning beefsteak filled the cabin. He chopped steadfastly and monotonously till the last case was finished.

Somebody knocked at the door, knocked again, and let himself in.

"What a mess!" he remarked, as he paused and surveyed the scene.

The severed eggs were beginning to thaw in the heat of the stove, and a miserable odor was growing stronger.

"Must a-happened on the steamer," he suggested.

Rasmunsen looked at him long and blankly.

"I'm Murray, Big Jim Murray, everybody knows me," the man volunteered. "I'm just hearin' your eggs is rotten, and I'm offerin' you two hundred for the batch. They ain't as good as salmon, but still they're fair scoffin's for dogs."

Rasmunsen seemed turned to stone. He did not move. "You go to hell," he said passionlessly.

"Now just consider. I pride myself it's a decent price for a mess like that, and it's better'n nothin'. Two hundred. What you say?"

"You go to hell," Rasmunsen repeated softly, "and get out of here."

Murray gaped with a great awe, then went out carefully, backward, with his eyes fixed on the other's face.

Rasmunsen followed him out and turned the dogs loose. He threw them all the salmon he had bought, and coiled a sled-lashing up in his hand. Then he reëntered the cabin and drew the latch in after him. The smoke from the cindered steak made his eyes smart. He stood on the bunk, passed the lashing over the ridge-pole, and measured the swing-off with his eye. It did not seem to satisfy, for he put the stool on the bunk and climbed upon the stool. He drove a noose in the end of the lashing and slipped his head through. The other end he made fast. Then he kicked the stool out from under.

BÂTARD

Bâtard was a devil. This was recognized throughout the Northland. "Hell's Spawn" he was called by many men, but his master, Black Leclère, chose for him the shameful name "Bâtard." Now Black Leclère was also a devil, and the twain were well matched. There is a saying that when two devils come together, hell is to pay. This is to be expected, and this certainly was to be expected when Bâtard and Black Leclère came together. The first time they met, Bâtard was a part-grown puppy, lean and hungry, with bitter eyes; and they met with snap and snarl, and wicked looks, for Leclère's upper lip had a wolfish way of lifting and showing the white, cruel teeth. And it lifted then, and his eyes glinted viciously, as he reached for Bâtard and dragged him out from the squirming litter. It was certain that they divined each other, for on the instant Bâtard had buried his puppy fangs in Leclère's hand, and Leclère, thumb and finger, was coolly choking his young life out of him.

"*Sacredam*," the Frenchman said softly, flirting the quick blood from his bitten hand and

127

gazing down on the little puppy choking and gasping in the snow.

Leclère turned to John Hamlin, storekeeper of the Sixty Mile Post. "Dat fo' w'at Ah lak heem. 'Ow moch, eh, you, *M'sieu'?* 'Ow moch? Ah buy heem, now; Ah buy heem queek."

And because he hated him with an exceeding bitter hate, Leclère bought Bâtard and gave him his shameful name. And for five years the twain adventured across the Northland, from St. Michael's and the Yukon delta to the head-reaches of the Pelly and even so far as the Peace River, Athabasca, and the Great Slave. And they acquired a reputation for uncompromising wickedness, the like of which never before attached itself to man and dog.

Bâtard did not know his father,—hence his name,—but, as John Hamlin knew, his father was a great gray timber wolf. But the mother of Bâtard, as he dimly remembered her, was snarling, bickering, obscene, husky, full-fronted and heavy-chested, with a malign eye, a cat-like grip on life, and a genius for trickery and evil. There was neither faith nor trust in her. Her treachery alone could be relied upon, and her wild-wood amours attested her general depravity. Much of evil and much of strength were there in these, Bâtard's progenitors, and, bone and flesh of their bone and flesh, he had inherited it all. And then came Black Leclère, to lay his heavy hand on the bit of pulsating puppy life, to press and prod and mould till it became a big bristling beast, acute in knavery, overspilling with hate, sinister, malignant, diabolical. With a proper

master Bâtard might have made an ordinary,
fairly efficient sled-dog He never got the
chance: Leclère but confirmed him in his con-
genital iniquity.

The history of Bâtard and Leclère is a history
of war—of five cruel, relentless years, of which
their first meeting is fit summary. To begin with,
it was Leclère's fault, for he hated with understanding and intelligence, while the long-
legged, ungainly puppy hated only blindly,
instinctively, without reason or method. At first
there were no refinements of cruelty (these
were to come later), but simple beatings and
crude brutalities. In one of these Bâtard had an
ear injured. He never regained control of the
riven muscles, and ever after the ear drooped
limply down to keep keen the memory of his
tormentor. And he never forgot.

His puppyhood was a period of foolish rebel-
lion. He was always worsted, but he fought
back because it was his nature to fight back.
And he was unconquerable. Yelping shrilly from
the pain of lash and club, he none the less contrived always to throw in the defiant snarl, the
bitter vindictive menace of his soul which
fetched without fail more blows and beatings.
But his was his mother's tenacious grip on life.
Nothing could kill him. He flourished under
misfortune, grew fat with famine, and out of
his terrible struggle for life developed a preter-
natural intelligence. His were the stealth and
cunning of the husky, his mother, and the
fierceness and valor of the wolf, his father.

Possibly it was because of his father that he

never wailed. His puppy yelps passed with his
lanky legs, so that he became grim and taciturn,
quick to strike, slow to warn. He answered curse
with snarl, and blow with snap, grinning the
while his implacable hatred; but never again,
under the extremest agony, did Leclère bring
from him the cry of fear nor of pain This
unconquerableness but fanned Leclère's wrath
and stirred him to greater deviltries.

Did Leclère give Bâtard half a fish and to his
mates whole ones, Bâtard went forth to rob
other dogs of their fish. Also he robbed cachés
and expressed himself in a thousand rogueries,
till he became a terror to all dogs and masters of
dogs. Did Leclère beat Bâtard and fondle Babette,—Babette who was not half the worker he
was,—why, Bâtard threw her down in the snow
and broke her hind leg in his heavy jaws, so that
Leclère was forced to shoot her. Likewise, in
bloody battles, Bâtard mastered all his team-
mates, set them the law of trail and forage, and
made them live to the law he set.

In five years he heard but one kind word, received but one soft stroke of a hand, and then
he did not know what manner of things they
were. He leaped like the untamed thing he was,
and his jaws were together in a flash. It was the
missionary at Sunrise, a newcomer in the country, who spoke the kind word and gave the soft
stroke of the hand. And for six months after, he
wrote no letters home to the States, and the surgeon at McQuestion travelled two hundred
miles on the ice to save him from blood-poison-
ing.

Men and dogs looked askance at Bâtard when he drifted into their camps and posts. The men greeted him with feet threateningly lifted for the kick, the dogs with bristling manes and bared fangs. Once a man did kick Bâtard, and Bâtard, with quick wolf snap, closed his jaws like a steel trap on the man's calf and crunched down to the bone. Whereat the man was determined to have his life, only Black Leclère, with ominous eyes and naked hunting-knife, stepped in between. The killing of Bâtard—ah, *sacredam, that* was a pleasure Leclère reserved for himself. Some day it would happen, or else—bah! who was to know? Anyway, the problem would be solved.

For they had become problems to each other. The very breath each drew was a challenge and a menace to the other. Their hate bound them together as love could never bind. Leclère was bent on the coming of the day when Bâtard should wilt in spirit and cringe and whimper at his feet. And Bâtard—Leclère knew what was in Bâtard's mind, and more than once had read it in Bâtard's eyes. And so clearly had he that when Bâtard was at his back, he made it a point to glance often over his shoulder.

Men marvelled when Leclère refused large money for the dog. "Some day you'll kill him and be out his price," said John Hamlin once, when Bâtard lay panting in the snow where Leclère had kicked him, and no one knew whether his ribs were broken, and no one dared look to see.

"Dat," said Leclère, dryly, "dat is my biz'ness, M'sieu'."

And the men marvelled that Bâtard did not run away. They did not understand. But Leclère understood. He was a man who lived much in the open, beyond the sound of human tongue, and he had learned the voices of wind and storm, the sigh of night, the whisper of dawn, the clash of day. In a dim way he could hear the green things growing, the running of the sap, the bursting of the bud. And he knew the subtle speech of the things that moved, of the rabbit in the snare, the moody raven beating the air with hollow wing, the baldface shuffling under the moon, the wolf like a gray shadow gliding betwixt the twilight and the dark. And to him Bâtard spoke clear and direct. Full well he understood why Bâtard did not run away, and he looked more often over his shoulder.

When in anger, Bâtard was not nice to look upon, and more than once had he leapt for Leclère's throat, to be stretched quivering and senseless in the snow, by the butt of the ever ready dogwhip. And so Bâtard learned to bide his time. When he reached his full strength and prime of youth, he thought the time had come. He was broad-chested, powerfully muscled, of far more than ordinary size, and his neck from head to shoulders was a mass of bristling hair—to all appearances a full-blooded wolf. Leclère was lying asleep in his furs when Bâtard deemed the time to be ripe. He crept upon him stealthily, head low to earth and lone ear laid back, with a feline softness of tread. Bâtard breathed gently, very gently, and not till he was close at hand did he raise his head. He paused for a moment, and looked at the bronzed bull throat, naked and knotty, and swelling to a deep and steady pulse. The slaver dripped down his fangs and slid off his tongue at the sight, and in that moment he remembered his drooping ear, his uncounted blows and prodigious wrongs, and without a sound sprang on the sleeping man.

Leclère awoke to the pang of the fangs in his throat, and, perfect animal that he was, he awoke clear-headed and with full comprehension. He closed on Bâtard's windpipe with both his hands, and rolled out of his furs to get his weight uppermost. But the thousands of Bâtard's ancestors had clung at the throats of unnumbered moose and caribou and dragged them down, and the wisdom of those ancestors was his. When Leclère's weight came on top of him, he drove his hind legs upward and in, and clawed down chest and abdomen, ripping and tearing through skin and muscle. And when he felt the man's body wince above him and lift, he worried and shook at the man's throat. His team-mates closed around in a snarling circle, and Bâtard, with failing breath and fading sense, knew that their jaws were hungry for him. But that did not matter—it was the man, the man above him, and he ripped and clawed, and shook and worried, to the last ounce of his strength. But Leclère choked him with both his hands, till Bâtard's chest heaved and writhed for the air denied, and his eyes glazed and set, and his jaws slowly loosened, and his tongue protruded black and swollen.

"Eh? *Bon*, you devil!" Leclère gurgled, mouth and throat clogged with his own blood, as he shoved the dizzy dog from him.

And then Leclère cursed the other dogs off as they fell upon Bâtard. They drew back into a wider circle, squatting alertly on their haunches and licking their chops, the hair on every neck bristling and erect

Bâtard recovered quickly, and at sound of Leclère's voice, tottered to his feet and swayed weakly back and forth.

"A-h-ah! You beeg devil!" Leclère spluttered. "Ah fix you; Ah fix you plentee, by *Gar!*"

Bâtard, the air biting into his exhausted lungs like wine, flashed full into the man's face, his jaws missing and coming together with a metallic clip. They rolled over and over on the snow, Leclère striking madly with his fists. Then they separated, face to face, and circled back and forth before each other. Leclère could have drawn his knife. His rifle was at his feet. But the beast in him was up and raging. He would do the thing with his hands—and his teeth. Bâtard sprang in, but Leclère knocked him over with a blow of the fist, fell upon him, and buried his teeth to the bone in the dog's shoulder.

It was a primordial setting and a primordial scene, such as might have been in the savage youth of the world. An open space in a dark forest, a ring of grinning wolf-dogs, and in the centre two beasts, locked in combat, snapping and snarling, raging madly about, panting, sobbing, cursing, straining, wild with passion, in a fury of murder, ripping and tearing and clawing in elemental brutishness.

But Leclère caught Bâtard behind the ear, with a blow from his fist, knocking him over, and, for the instant, stunning him. Then Leclère leaped upon him with his feet, and sprang up and down, striving to grind him into the earth. Both Bâtard's hind legs were broken ere Leclère ceased that he might catch breath.

"A-a-ah! A-a-ah!" he screamed, incapable of speech, shaking his fist, through sheer impotence of throat and larynx.

But Bâtard was indomitable. He lay there in a helpless welter, his lip feebly lifting and writhing to the snarl he had not the strength to utter. Leclère kicked him, and the tired jaws closed on the ankle, but could not break the skin.

Then Leclère picked up the whip and proceeded almost to cut him to pieces, at each stroke of the lash crying: "Dis taim Ah break you! Eh? By *Gar!* Ah break you!"

In the end, exhausted, fainting from loss of blood, he crumpled up and fell by his victim, and when the wolf-dogs closed in to take their vengeance, with his last consciousness dragged his body on top Bâtard to shield him from their fangs.

This occurred not far from Sunrise, and the missionary, opening the door to Leclère a few hours later, was surprised to note the absence of Bâtard from the team. Nor did his surprise

lessen when Leclère threw back the robes from
the sled, gathered Bâtard into his arms, and
staggered across the threshold. It happened
that the surgeon of McQuestion, who was something of a gadabout, was up on a gossip, and between them they proceeded to repair Leclère.

"*Merci, non,*" said he. "Do you fix firs' de dog.
To die? *Non.* Eet is not good. Becos' heem Ah
mus' yet break. Dat fo' w'at he mus' not die."

The surgeon called it a marvel, the missionary
a miracle, that Leclère pulled through at all;
and so weakened was he, that in the spring the
fever got him, and he went on his back again.
Bâtard had been in even worse plight; but his
grip on life prevailed, and the bones of his hind
legs knit, and his organs righted themselves,
during the several weeks he lay strapped to the
floor. And by the time Leclère, finally conva-
lescent, sallow and shaky, took the sun by the
cabin door, Bâtard had reasserted his supremacy among his kind, and brought not only his
own team-mates but the missionary's dogs into
subjection.

He moved never a muscle, nor twitched a
hair, when, for the first time, Leclère tottered
out on the missionary's arm, and sank down
slowly and with infinite caution on the three-
legged stool.

"*Bon!*" he said. "*Bon!* De good sun!" And he
stretched out his wasted hands and washed
them in the warmth

Then his gaze fell on the dog, and the old
light blazed back in his eyes. He touched the
missionary lightly on the arm. "*Mon père,* dat is

one beeg devil, dat Bâtard. You will bring me one pistol, so, dat Ah drínk de sun in peace."

And thenceforth for many days he sat in the sun before the cabin door. He never dozed, and the pistol lay always across his knees. Bâtard had a way, the first thing each day, of looking for the weapon in its wonted place. At sight of it he would lift his lip faintly in token that he understood, and Leclère would lift his own lip in an answering grin. One day the missionary took note of the trick.

"Bless me!" he said. "I really believe the brute comprehends."

Leclère laughed softly. "Look you, *mon père.* Dat w'at Ah now spik, to dat does he lissen."

As if in confirmation, Bâtard just perceptibly wriggled his lone ear up to catch the sound.

"Ah say 'keel.' "

Bâtard growled deep down in his throat, the hair bristled along his neck, and every muscle went tense and expectant.

"Ah lift de gun, so, like dat." And suiting action to word, he sighted the pistol at Bâtard.

Bâtard, with a single leap, sideways, landed around the corner of the cabin out of sight.

"Bless me!" he repeated at intervals.

Leclère grinned proudly.

"But why does he not run away?"

The Frenchman's shoulders went up in the racial shrug that means all things from total ignorance to infinite understanding.

"Then why do you not kill him?"

Again the shoulders went up.

"*Mon père,*" he said after a pause, "de taim is

not yet. He is one beeg devil. Some taim Ah break heem, so, an' so, all to leetle bits. Hey? Some taim. *Bon!*"

A day came when Leclère gathered his dogs together and floated down in a bateau to Forty Mile, and on to the Porcupine, where he took a commission from the P. C. Company, and went exploring for the better part of a year. After that he poled up the Koyokuk to deserted Arctic City, and later came drifting back, from camp to camp, along the Yukon. And during the long months Bâtard was well lessoned. He learned many tortures, and, notably, the torture of hunger, the torture of thirst, the torture of fire, and, worst of all, the torture of music

Like the rest of his kind, he did not enjoy music. It gave him exquisite anguish, racking him nerve by nerve, and ripping apart every fibre of his being. It made him howl, long and wolf-like, as when the wolves bay the stars on frosty nights. He could not help howling. It was his one weakness in the contest with Leclère, and it was his shame. Leclère, on the other hand, passionately loved music—as passionately as he loved strong drink. And when his soul clamored for expression, it usually uttered itself in one or the other of the two ways, and more usually in both ways. And when he had drunk, his brain a-lilt with unsung song and the devil in him aroused and rampant, his soul found its supreme utterance in torturing Bâtard.

"Now we will haf a leetle museek," he would say. "Eh? W'at you t'ink, Bâtard?"

It was only an old and battered harmonica,

tenderly treasured and patiently repaired; but it was the best that money could buy, and out of its silver reeds he drew weird vagrant airs that men had never heard before. Then Bâtard, dumb of throat, with teeth tight clenched, would back away, inch by inch, to the farthest cabin corner. And Leclère, playing, playing, a stout club tucked under his arm, followed the animal up, inch by inch, step by step, till there was no further retreat.

At first Bâtard would crowd himself into the smallest possible space, grovelling close to the floor; but as the music came nearer and nearer, he was forced to uprear, his back jammed into the logs, his fore legs fanning the air as though to beat off the rippling waves of sound. He still kept his teeth together, but severe muscular contractions attacked his body, strange twitchings and jerkings, till he was all a-quiver and writhing in silent torment. As he lost control, his jaws spasmodically wrenched apart, and deep throaty vibrations issued forth, too low in the register of sound for human ear to catch. And then, nostrils distended, eyes dilated, hair bristling in helpless rage, arose the long wolf howl. It came with a slurring rush upward, swelling to a great heart-breaking burst of sound, and dying away in sadly cadenced woe—then the next rush upward, octave upon octave; the bursting heart; and the infinite sorrow and misery, fainting, fading, falling, and dying slowly away

It was fit for hell. And Leclère, with fiendish ken, seemed to divine each particular nerve and

heartstring, and with long wails and tremblings
and sobbing minors to make it yield up its last
shred of grief. It was frightful, and for twenty-
four hours after, Bâtard was nervous and un-
strung, starting at common sounds, tripping
over his own shadow, but, withal, vicious and
masterful with his team-mates. Nor did he show
signs of a breaking spirit. Rather did he grow
more grim and taciturn, biding his time with an
inscrutable patience that began to puzzle and
weigh upon Leclère. The dog would lie in the
firelight, motionless, for hours, gazing straight
before him at Leclère, and hating him with his
bitter eyes.

Often the man felt that he had bucked
against the very essence of life—the unconquerable essence that swept the hawk down out of
the sky like a feathered thunderbolt, that drove
the great gray goose across the zones, that
hurled the spawning salmon through two thousand miles of boiling Yukon flood. At such times
he felt impelled to express his own unconquerable essence; and with strong drink, wild music,
and Bâtard, he indulged in vast orgies, wherein
he pitted his puny strength in the face of things,
and challenged all that was, and had been, and
was yet to be.

"Dere is somet'ing dere," he affirmed, when
the rhythmed vagaries of his mind touched the
secret chords of Bâtard's being and brought
forth the long lugubrious howl. "Ah pool eet out
wid bot' my han's, so, an' so. Ha! Ha! Eet is
fonee! Eet is ver' fonee! De priest chant, de
womans pray, de mans swear, de leetle bird go

peep-peep, Bâtard, heem go *yow-yow*—an' eet is all de ver' same t'ing. Ha! Ha!."

Father Gautier, a worthy priest, once reproved him with instances of concrete perdition. He never reproved him again.

"Eet may be so, *mon père*," he made answer. "An' Ah t'ink Ah go troo hell a-snappin', lak de hemlock troo de fire. Eh, *mon père?*"

But all bad things come to an end as well as good, and so with Black Leclère. On the summer low water, in a poling boat, he left McDougall for Sunrise. He left McDougall in company with Timothy Brown, and arrived at Sunrise by himself. Further, it was known that they had quarrelled just previous to pulling out; for the *Lizzie*, a wheezy ten-ton sternwheeler, twenty-four hours behind, beat Leclère in by three days. And when he did get in, it was with a clean-drilled bullet-hole through his shoulder muscle, and a tale of ambush and murder.

A strike had been made at Sunrise, and things had changed considerably. With the infusion of several hundred gold-seekers, a deal of whiskey, and half a dozen equipped gamblers, the missionary had seen the page of his years of labor with the Indians wiped clean. When the squaws became preoccupied with cooking beans and keeping the fire going for the wifeless miners, and the bucks with swapping their warm furs for black bottles and broken timepieces, he took to his bed, said "bless me" several times, and departed to his final accounting in a rough-hewn, oblong box. Whereupon the gamblers moved their roulette and faro tables into the mission house, and the click of chips and clink of glasses went up from dawn till dark and to dawn again.

Now Timothy Brown was well beloved among these adventurers of the north. The one thing against him was his quick temper and ready fist,—a little thing, for which his kind heart and forgiving hand more than atoned. On the other hand, there was nothing to atone for Black Leclère. He was "black," as more than one remembered deed bore witness, while he was as well hated as the other was beloved. So the men of Sunrise put an antiseptic dressing on his shoulder and haled him before Judge Lynch.

It was a simple affair. He had quarrelled with Timothy Brown at McDougall. With Timothy Brown he had left McDougall. Without Timothy Brown he had arrived at Sunrise. Considered in the light of his evilness, the unanimous conclusion was that he had killed Timothy Brown. On the other hand, Leclère acknowledged their facts, but challenged their conclusion, and gave his own explanation. Twenty miles out of Sunrise he and Timothy Brown were poling the boat along the rocky shore. From that shore two rifle-shots rang out. Timothy Brown pitched out of the boat and went down bubbling red, and that was the last of Timothy Brown. He, Leclère, pitched into the bottom of the boat with a stinging shoulder. He lay very quiet, peeping at the shore. After a time two Indians stuck up their heads and came out to the water's edge, carrying between them a birch-bark canoe. As they launched it, Leclère let fly. He potted one, who went over the side after the manner of Timothy Brown. The other dropped into the bottom of the canoe, and then canoe and poling boat went down the stream in a drifting battle. After that they hung up on a split current, and the canoe passed on one side of an island the poling boat on the other. That was the last of the canoe, and he came on into Sunrise. Yes, from the way the Indian in the canoe jumped, he was sure he had potted him. That was all.

This explanation was not deemed adequate. They gave him ten hours' grace while the *Lizzie* steamed down to investigate. Ten hours later she came wheezing back to Sunrise. There had been nothing to investigate. No evidence had been found to back up his statements. They told him to make his will, for he possessed a fifty-thousand-dollar Sunrise claim, and they were a law-abiding as well as a law-giving breed.

Leclère shrugged his shoulders. "Bot one t'ing," he said; "a leetle, w'at you call, favor—a leetle favor, dat is eet. I gif my feefty t'ousan' dollair to de church. I gif my husky dog, Bâtard, to de devil. De leetle favor? Firs' you hang heem, an' den you hang me. Eet is good, eh?"

Good it was, they agreed, that Hell's Spawn should break trail for his master across the last divide, and the court was adjourned down to the river bank, where a big spruce tree stood by

itself. Slackwater Charley put a hangman's knot
in the end of a hauling-line, and the noose was
slipped over Leclère's head and pulled tight
around his neck. His hands were tied behind
his back, and he was assisted to the top of a
cracker box. Then the running end of the line
was passed over an overhanging branch, drawn
taut, and made fast. To kick the box out from
under would leave him dancing on the air.

"Now for the dog," said Webster Shaw,
sometime mining engineer. "You'll have to rope
him, Slackwater."

Leclère grinned. Slackwater took a chew of
tobacco, rove a running noose, and proceeded
leisurely to coil a few turns in his hand. He
paused once or twice to brush particularly offensive mosquitoes from off his face. Everybody
was brushing mosquitoes, except Leclère, about
whose head a small cloud was visible. Even
Bâtard, lying full-stretched on the ground, with
his fore paws rubbed the pests away from eyes
and mouth.

But while Slackwater waited for Bâtard to
lift his head, a faint call came down the quiet
air, and a man was seen waving his arms and
running across the flat from Sunrise. It was the
storekeeper.

"C-call 'er off, boys," he panted, as he came
in among them.

"Little Sandy and Bernadotte's jes' got in,"
he explained with returning breath. "Landed
down below an' come up by the short cut. Got
the Beaver with 'm. Picked 'm up in his canoe,
stuck in a back channel, with a couple of bullet

holes in 'm. Other buck was Klok-Kutz, the one that knocked spots out of his squaw and dusted."

"Eh? W'at Ah say? Eh?" Leclère cried exultantly. "Dat de one fo' sure! Ah know. Ah spik true."

"The thing to do is teach these damned Siwashes a little manners," spoke Webster Shaw. "They're getting fat and sassy, and we'll have to bring them down a peg. Round in all the bucks and string up the Beaver for an object lesson. That's the programme. Come on and let's see what he's got to say for himself."

"Heh, M'sieu'!" Leclère called, as the crowd began to melt away through the twilight in the direction of Sunrise. "Ah lak ver' moch to see de fon."

"Oh, we'll turn you loose when we come back," Webster Shaw shouted over his shoulder. "In the meantime meditate on your sins and the ways of providence. It will do you good, so be grateful."

As is the way with men who are accustomed to great hazards, whose nerves are healthy and trained to patience, so it was with Leclére, who settled himself to the long wait——which is to say that he reconciled his mind to it. There was no settling of the body, for the taut rope forced him to stand rigidly erect. The least relaxation of the leg muscles pressed the rough-fibred noose into his neck, while the upright position caused him much pain in his wounded shoulder. He projected his under lip and expelled his breath upward along his face to blow the mosquitoes away from his eyes. But the situation had its compensation. To be snatched from the maw of death was well worth a little bodily suffering, only it was unfortunate that he should miss the hanging of the Beaver.

And so he mused, till his eyes chanced to fall upon Bâtard, head between fore paws and stretched on the ground asleep. And then Leclére ceased to muse. He studied the animal closely, striving to sense if the sleep were real or feigned. Bâtard's sides were heaving regularly, but Leclère felt that the breath came and went a shade too quickly; also he felt that there was a vigilance or alertness to every hair that belied unshackling sleep. He would have given his Sunrise claim to be assured that the dog was not awake, and once, when one of his joints cracked, he looked quickly and guiltily at Bâtard to see if he roused. He did not rouse then, but a few minutes later he got up slowly and lazily, stretched, and looked carefully about him.

"*Sacredam*," said Leclère, under his breath. Assured that no one was in sight or hearing, Bâtard sat down, curled his upper lip almost into a smile, looked up at Leclère, and licked his chops.

"Ah see my feenish," the man said, and laughed sardonically aloud.

Bâtard came nearer, the useless ear wabbling, the good ear cocked forward with devilish comprehension. He thrust his head on one side quizzically, and advanced with mincing, playful steps. He rubbed his body gently against the box till it shook and shook again. Leclère teetered carefully to maintain his equilibrium.

"Bâtard," he said calmly, "look out. Ah keel you."

Bâtard snarled at the word, and shook the box with greater force. Then he upreared, and with his fore paws threw his weight against it higher up. Leclère kicked out with one foot, but the rope bit into his neck and checked so abruptly as nearly to overbalance him.

"Hi, ya! *Chook! Mush-on!*" he screamed.

Bâtard retreated, for twenty feet or so, with a fiendish levity in his bearing that Leclère could not mistake. He remembered the dog often breaking the scum of ice on the water hole, by lifting up and throwing his weight upon it; and, remembering, he understood what he now had in mind. Bâtard faced about and paused. He showed his white teeth in a grin, which Leclère answered; and then hurled his body through the air, in full charge, straight for the box.

Fifteen minutes later, Slackwater Charley and Webster Shaw, returning, caught a glimpse of a ghostly pendulum swinging back and forth in the dim light. As they hurriedly drew in closer, they made out the man's inert body, and a live thing that clung to it, and shook and worried, and gave to it the swaying motion.

"Hi, ya! *Chook!* you Spawn of Hell," yelled Webster Shaw.

But Bâtard glared at him, and snarled threateningly, without loosing his jaws.

Slackwater Charley got out his revolver, but his hand was shaking, as with a chill, and he fumbled.

"Here, you take it," he said, passing the weapon over.

Webster Shaw laughed shortly, drew a sight between the gleaming eyes, and pressed the trigger. Bâtard's body twitched with the shock, threshed the ground spasmodically for a moment, and went suddenly limp. But his teeth still held fast locked.

THE DOMINANT
PRIMORDIAL BEAST

THE DOMINANT PRIMORDIAL beast was strong
in Buck, and under the fierce conditions of trail
life it grew and grew. Yet it was a secret
growth. His new-born cunning gave him poise
and control. He was too busy adjusting himself
to the new life to feel at ease, and not only did
he not pick fights, but he avoided them whenever possible. A certain deliberateness characterized his attitude. He was not prone to
rashness and precipitate action; and in the bitter hatred between him and Spitz he betrayed
no impatience, shunned all offensive acts.

On the other hand, possibly because he
divined in Buck a dangerous rival, Spitz never
lost an opportunity of showing his teeth. He
even went out of his way to bully Buck, striving
constantly to start the fight which could end
only in the death of one or the other.

Early in the trip this might have taken place
had it not been for an unwonted accident. At
the end of this day they made a bleak and
miserable camp on the shore of Lake Le Barge.

Driving snow, a wind that cut like a white-hot knife, and darkness, had forced them to grope for a camping place. They could hardly have fared worse. At their backs rose a perpendicular wall of rock, and Perrault and François were compelled to make their fire and spread their sleeping robes on the ice of the lake itself. The tent they had discarded at Dyea in order to travel light. A few sticks of driftwood furnished them with a fire that thawed down through the ice and left them to eat supper in the dark.

Close in under the sheltering rock Buck made his nest. So snug and warm was it, that he was loath to leave it when François distributed the fish which he had first thawed over the fire. But when Buck finished his ration and returned, he found his nest occupied. A warning snarl told him that the trespasser was Spitz. Till now Buck had avoided trouble with his enemy, but this was too much. The beast in him roared. He sprang upon Spitz with a fury which surprised them both, and Spitz particularly, for his whole experience with Buck had gone to teach him that his rival was an unusually timid dog, who managed to hold his own only because of his great weight and size.

François was surprised, too, when they shot out in a tangle from the disrupted nest and he divined the cause of the trouble. "A-a-ah!" he cried to Buck. "Gif it to heem, by Gar! Gif it to heem, the dirty t'eef!"

Spitz was equally willing. He was crying with sheer rage and eagerness as he circled back and forth for a chance to spring in. Buck was no less eager, and no less cautious, as he likewise circled back and forth for the advantage. But it was then that the unexpected happened, the thing which projected their struggle for supremacy far into the future, past many a weary mile of trail and toil.

An oath from Perrault, the resounding impact of a club upon a bony frame, and a shrill yelp of pain, heralded the breaking forth of pandemonium. The camp was suddenly discovered to be alive with skulking furry forms,—starving huskies, four or five score of them, who had scented the camp from some Indian village. They had crept in while Buck and Spitz were fighting, and when the two men sprang among them with stout clubs they showed their teeth and fought back. They were crazed by the smell of the food. Perrault found one with head buried in the grub-box. His club landed heavily on the gaunt ribs, and the grub-box was capsized on the ground. On the instant a score of the famished brutes were scrambling for the bread and bacon. The clubs fell upon them unheeded. They yelped and howled under the rain of blows, but struggled none the less madly till the last crumb had been devoured.

In the meantime the astonished team-dogs had burst out of their nests only to be set upon by the fierce invaders. Never had Buck seen such dogs. It seemed as though their bones would burst through their skins. They were mere skeletons, draped loosely in draggled

hides, with blazing eyes and slavered fangs.
But the hunger-madness made them terrifying,
irresistible. There was no opposing them. The
team-dogs were swept back against the cliff at
the first onset. Buck was beset by three huskies,
and in a trice his head and shoulders were
ripped and slashed. The din was frightful.
Billee was crying as usual. Dave and Sol-leks,
dripping blood from a score of wounds, were
fighting bravely side by side. Joe was snapping
like a demon. Once, his teeth closed on the fore
leg of a husky, and he crunched down through
the bone. Pike, the malingerer, leaped upon the
crippled animal, breaking its neck with a quick
flash of teeth and a jerk. Buck got a frothing
adversary by the throat, and was sprayed with
blood when his teeth sank through the jugular.
The warm taste of it in his mouth goaded him
to greater fierceness. He flung himself upon another, and at the same time felt teeth sink into
his own throat. It was Spitz, treacherously at-
tacking from the side.

Perrault and François, having cleaned out
their part of the camp, hurried to save their
sled-dogs. The wild wave of famished beasts
rolled back before them, and Buck shook himself free. But it was only for a moment. The two
men were compelled to run back to save the
grub, upon which the huskies returned to the
attack on the team. Billee, terrified into brav-
ery, sprang through the savage circle and fled
away over the ice. Pike and Dub followed on
his heels, with the rest of the team behind. As
Buck drew himself together to spring after

them, out of the tail of his eye he saw Spitz rush upon him, with the evident intention of overthrowing him. Once off his feet and under that mass of huskies, there was no hope for him. But he braced himself to the shock of Spitz's charge, then joined the flight out on the lake.

Later, the nine team-dogs gathered together and sought shelter in the forest. Though unpursued, they were in a sorry plight. There was not one who was not wounded in four or five places, while some were wounded grievously. Dub was badly injured in a hind leg; Dolly, the last husky added to the team at Dyea, had a badly torn throat; Joe had lost an eye; while Billee, the good-natured, with an ear chewed and rent to ribbons, cried and whimpered throughout the night. At daybreak they limped warily back to camp, to find the marauders gone and the two men in bad tempers. Fully half their grub supply was gone. The huskies had chewed through the sled lashings and canvas coverings. In fact, nothing, no matter how remotely eatable, had escaped them. They had eaten a pair of Perrault's moose-hide moccasins, chunks out of the leather traces, and even two feet of lash from the end of François's whip. He broke from a mournful contemplation of it to look over his wounded dogs.

"Ah, my frien's," he said softly, "mebbe it mek you mad dog, dose many bites. Mebbe all mad dog, sacredam! Wot you t'ink, eh, Perrault?"

The courier shook his head dubiously. With

four hundred miles of trail still between him and Dawson, he could ill afford to have madness break out among his dogs. Two hours of cursing and exertion got the harnesses into shape, and the wound-stiffened team was under way, struggling painfully over the hardest part of the trail they had yet encountered, and for that matter, the hardest between them and Dawson.

The Thirty Mile River was wide open. Its wild water defied the frost, and it was in the eddies only and in the quiet places that the ice held at all. Six days of exhausting toil were required to cover those thirty terrible miles. And terrible they were, for every foot of them was accomplished at the risk of life to dog and man. A dozen times, Perrault, nosing the way, broke through the ice bridges, being saved by the long pole he carried, which he so held that it fell each time across the hole made by his body. But a cold snap was on, the thermometer registering fifty below zero, and each time he broke through he was compelled for very life to build a fire and dry his garments.

Nothing daunted him. It was because nothing daunted him that he had been chosen for government courier. He took all manner of risks, resolutely thrusting his little weazened face into the frost and struggling on from dim dawn to dark. He skirted the frowning shores on rim ice that bent and crackled under foot and upon which they dared not halt. Once, the sled broke through, with Dave and Buck, and they were half-frozen and all but drowned by the time they were dragged out. The usual fire was necessary to save them. They were coated solidly with ice, and the two men kept them on the run around the fire, sweating and thawing, so close that they were singed by the flames.

At another time Spitz went through, dragging the whole team after him up to Buck, who strained backward with all his strength, his fore paws on the slippery edge and the ice quivering and snapping all around. But behind him was Dave, likewise straining backward, and behind the sled was François, pulling till his tendons cracked.

Again, the rim ice broke away before and behind, and there was no escape except up the cliff. Perrault scaled it by a miracle, while François prayed for just that miracle; and with every thong and sled lashing and the last bit of harness rove into a long rope, the dogs were hoisted, one by one, to the cliff crest. François came up last, after the sled and load. Then came the search for a place to descend, which descent was ultimately made by the aid of the rope, and night found them back on the river with a quarter of a mile to the day's credit.

By the time they made the Hootalinqua and good ice, Buck was played out. The rest of the dogs were in like condition; but Perrault, to make up lost time, pushed them late and early. The first day they covered thirty-five miles to the Big Salmon; the next day thirty-five more to the Little Salmon; the third day forty miles, which brought them well up toward the Five Fingers.

Buck's feet were not so compact and hard as the feet of the huskies. He had softened during the many generations since the day his last wild ancestor was tamed by a cave-dweller or river man. All day long he limped in agony, and camp once made, lay down like a dead dog. Hungry as he was, he would not move to receive his ration of fish, which François had to bring to him. Also, the dog-driver rubbed Buck's feet for half an hour each night after supper, and sacrificed the tops of his own moccasins to make four moccasins for Buck. This was a great relief, and Buck caused even the weazened face of Perrault to twist itself into a grin one morning, when François forgot the moccasins and Buck lay on his back, his four feet waving appealingly in the air, and refused to budge without them. Later his feet grew hard to the trail, and the worn-out foot-gear was thrown away.

At the Pelly one morning, as they were harnessing up, Dolly, who had never been conspicuous for anything, went suddenly mad. She announced her condition by a long, heartbreaking wolf howl that sent every dog bristling with fear, then sprang straight for Buck. He had never seen a dog go mad, nor did he have any reason to fear madness; yet he knew that here was horror, and fled away from it in a panic. Straight away he raced, with Dolly, panting and frothing, one leap behind; nor could she gain on him, so great was his terror, nor could he leave her, so great was her madness. He plunged through the wooded breast of the island, fled down to the lower end, crossed a back channel filled with rough ice to another island, gained a third island, curved back to the main river, and in desperation started to cross it. And all the time, though he did not look, he could hear her snarling just one leap behind. François called to him a quarter of a mile away and he doubled back, still one leap ahead, gasping painfully for air and putting all his faith in that François would save him. The dog-driver held the axe poised in his hand, and as Buck shot past him the axe crashed down upon mad Dolly's head.

Buck staggered over against the sled, exhausted, sobbing for breath, helpless. This was Spitz's opportunity. He sprang upon Buck, and twice his teeth sank into his unresisting foe and ripped and tore the flesh to the bone. Then François's lash descended, and Buck had the satisfaction of watching Spitz receive the worst whipping as yet administered to any of the team.

"One devil, dat Spitz," remarked Perrault. "Some dam day heem keel dat Buck."

"Dat Buck two devils," was François's rejoinder. "All de tam I watch dat Buck I know for sure. Lissen: some dam fine day heem get mad lak hell an' den heem chew dat Spitz all up an' spit heem out on de snow. Sure. I know."

From then on it was war between them. Spitz, as lead-dog and acknowledged master of the team, felt his supremacy threatened by this strange Southland dog. And strange Buck was to him, for of the many Southland dogs he had known, not one had shown up worthily in camp and on trail. They were all too soft, dying under the toil, the frost, and starvation. Buck was the exception. He alone endured and prospered, matching the husky in strength, savagery, and cunning. Then he was a masterful dog, and what made him dangerous was the fact that the club of the man in the red sweater had knocked all blind pluck and rashness out of his desire for mastery. He was preëminently cunning, and could bide his time with a patience that was nothing less than primitive.

It was inevitable that the clash for leadership should come. Buck wanted it. He wanted it because it was his nature, because he had been gripped tight by that nameless, incomprehensible pride of the trail and trace—that pride which holds dogs in the toil to the last gasp, which lures them to die joyfully in the harness, and breaks their hearts if they are cut out of the harness. This was the pride of Dave as wheel-dog, of Sol-leks as he pulled with all his strength; the pride that laid hold of them at break of camp, transforming them from sour and sullen brutes into straining, eager, ambitious creatures; the pride that spurred them on all day and dropped them at pitch of camp at night, letting them fall back into gloomy unrest and uncontent. This was the pride that bore up Spitz and made him thrash the sled-dogs who blundered and shirked in the traces or hid away at harness-up time in the morning. Likewise it was this pride that made him fear Buck as a possible lead-dog. And this was Buck's pride, too.

He openly threatened the other's leadership. He came between him and the shirks he should have punished. And he did it deliberately. One night there was a heavy snowfall, and in the morning Pike, the malingerer, did not appear. He was securely hidden in his nest under a foot of snow. François called him and sought him in vain. Spitz was wild with wrath. He raged through the camp, smelling and digging in every likely place, snarling so frightfully that Pike heard and shivered in his hiding-place.

But when he was at last unearthed, and Spitz flew at him to punish him, Buck flew, with equal rage, in between. So unexpected was it, and so shrewdly managed, that Spitz was hurled backward and off his feet. Pike, who had been trembling abjectly, took heart at this open mutiny, and sprang upon his overthrown leader. Buck, to whom fair-play was a forgotten code, likewise sprang upon Spitz. But François, chuckling at the incident while unswerving in the administration of justice, brought his lash down upon Buck with all his might. This failed to drive Buck from his prostrate rival, and the butt of the whip was brought intó play. Half-stunned by the blow, Buck was knocked backward and the lash laid upon him again and again, while Spitz soundly punished the many times offending Pike.

In the days that followed, as Dawson grew closer and closer, Buck still continued to interfere between Spitz and the culprits; but he did

it craftily, when François was not around. With
the covert mutiny of Buck, a general insubordi-
nation sprang up and increased. Dave and Sol-
leks were unaffected, but the rest of the team
went from bad to worse. Things no longer went
right. There was continual bickering and jan-
gling. Trouble was always afoot, and at the
bottom of it was Buck. He kept François busy,
for the dog-driver was in constant apprehen-
sion of the life-and-death struggle between the
two which he knew must take place sooner or
later; and on more than one night the sounds of
quarrelling and strife among the other dogs
turned him out of his sleeping robe, fearful that
Buck and Spitz were at it.

But the opportunity did not present itself,
and they pulled into Dawson one dreary afternoon with the great fight still to come. Here
were many men, and countless dogs, and Buck
found them all at work. It seemed the ordained
order of things that dogs should work. All day
they swung up and down the main street in
long teams, and in the night their jingling bells
still went by. They hauled cabin logs and firewood, freighted up to the mines, and did all
manner of work that horses did in the Santa
Clara Valley. Here and there Buck met Southland dogs, but in the main they were the wild
wolf husky breed. Every night, regularly, at
nine, at twelve, at three, they lifted a nocturnal
song, a weird and eerie chant, in which it was
Buck's delight to join.

With the aurora borealis flaming coldly overhead, or the stars leaping in the frost dance,

and the land numb and frozen under its pall of snow, this song of the huskies might have been the defiance of life, only it was pitched in minor key, with long-drawn wailings and half-sobs, and was more the pleading of life, the articulate travail of existence. It was an old song, old as the breed itself—one of the first songs of the younger world in a day when songs were sad. It was invested with the woe of unnumbered generations, this plaint by which Buck was so strangely stirred. When he moaned and sobbed, it was with the pain of living that was of old the pain of his wild fathers, and the fear and mystery of the cold and dark that was to them fear and mystery. And that he should be stirred by it marked the completeness with which he harked back through the ages of fire and roof to the raw beginnings of life in the howling ages.

Seven days from the time they pulled into Dawson, they dropped down the steep bank by the Barracks to the Yukon Trail, and pulled for Dyea and Salt Water. Perrault was carrying despatches if anything more urgent than those he had brought in; also, the travel pride had gripped him, and he purposed to make the record trip of the year. Several things favored him in this. The week's rest had recuperated the dogs and put them in thorough trim. The trail they had broken into the country was packed hard by later journeyers. And further, the police had arranged in two or three places deposits of grub for dog and man, and he was travelling light.

They made Sixty Mile, which is a fifty-mile run, on the first day; and the second day saw them booming up the Yukon well on their way to Pelly. But such splendid running was achieved not without great trouble and vexation on the part of François. The insidious revolt led by Buck had destroyed the solidarity of the team. It no longer was as one dog leaping in the traces. The encouragement Buck gave the rebels led them into all kinds of petty misdemeanors. No more was Spitz a leader greatly to be feared. The old awe departed, and they grew equal to challenging his authority. Pike robbed him of half a fish one night, and gulped it down under the protection of Buck. Another night Dub and Joe fought Spitz and made him forego the punishment they deserved. And even Billee, the good-natured, was less good-natured, and whined not half so placatingly as in former days. Buck never came near Spitz without snarling and bristling menacingly. In fact, his conduct approached that of a bully, and he was given to swaggering up and down before Spitz's very nose.

The breaking down of discipline likewise affected the dogs in their relations with one another. They quarrelled and bickered more than ever among themselves, till at times the camp was a howling bedlam. Dave and Sol-leks alone were unaltered, though they were made irritable by the unending squabbling. François swore strange barbarous oaths, and stamped the snow in futile rage, and tore his hair. His lash was always singing among the dogs, but it was of small avail. Directly his back was turned they were at it again. He backed up Spitz with his whip, while Buck backed up the remainder of the team. François knew he was behind all the trouble, and Buck knew he knew; but Buck was too clever ever again to be caught red-handed. He worked faithfully in the harness, for the toil had become a delight to him; yet it was a greater delight slyly to precipitate a fight amongst his mates and tangle the traces.

At the mouth of the Tahkeena, one night after supper, Dub turned up a snowshoe rabbit, blundered it, and missed. In a second the whole team was in full cry. A hundred yards away was a camp of the Northwest Police, with fifty dogs, huskies all, who joined the chase. The rabbit sped down the river, turned off into a small creek, up the frozen bed of which it held steadily. It ran lightly on the surface of the snow, while the dogs ploughed through by main strength. Buck led the pack, sixty strong, around bend after bend, but he could not gain. He lay down low to the race, whining eagerly, his splendid body flashing forward, leap by leap, in the wan white moonlight. And leap by leap, like some pale frost wraith, the snowshoe rabbit flashed on ahead.

All that stirring of old instincts which at stated periods drives men out from the sounding cities to forest and plain to kill things by chemically propelled leaden pellets, the blood lust, the joy to kill—all this was Buck's, only it was infinitely more intimate. He was ranging at the head of the pack, running the wild thing down, the living meat, to kill with his own teeth and wash his muzzle to the eyes in warm blood.

There is an ecstasy that marks the summit of life, and beyond which life cannot rise. And such is the paradox of living, this ecstasy comes when one is most alive, and it comes as a complete forgetfulness that one is alive. This ecstasy, this forgetfulness of living, comes to the artist, caught up and out of himself in a sheet of flame; it comes to the soldier, war-mad on a stricken field and refusing quarter; and it came to Buck, leading the pack, sounding the old wolf-cry, straining after the food that was alive and that fled swiftly before him through the moonlight. He was sounding the deeps of his nature, and of the parts of his nature that were deeper than he, going back into the womb of Time. He was mastered by the sheer surging of life, the tidal wave of being, the perfect joy of each separate muscle, joint, and sinew in that it was everything that was not death, that it was aglow and rampant, expressing itself in movement, flying exultantly under the stars and over the face of dead matter that did not move.

But Spitz, cold and calculating even in his supreme moods, left the pack and cut across a narrow neck of land where the creek made a long bend around. Buck did not know of this, and as he rounded the bend, the frost wraith of a rabbit still flitting before him, he saw another and larger frost wraith leap from the overhanging bank into the immediate path of the rabbit.

It was Spitz. The rabbit could not turn, and as
the white teeth broke its back in mid air it
shrieked as loudly as a stricken man may
shriek. At sound of this, the cry of Life plunging down from Life's apex in the grip of Death,
the full pack at Buck's heels raised a hell's
chorus of delight.

Buck did not cry out. He did not check himself, but drove in upon Spitz, shoulder to shoulder, so hard that he missed the throat. They
rolled over and over in the powdery snow.
Spitz gained his feet almost as though he had
not been overthrown, slashing Buck down the
shoulder and leaping clear. Twice his teeth
clipped together, like the steel jaws of a trap, as
he backed away for better footing, with lean
and lifting lips that writhed and snarled.

In a flash Buck knew it. The time had come.
It was to the death. As they circled about, snarling, ears laid back, keenly watchful for the advantage, the scene came to Buck with a sense of
familiarity. He seemed to remember it all,—the
white woods, and earth, and moonlight, and
the thrill of battle. Over the whiteness and
silence brooded a ghostly calm. There was not
the faintest whisper of air—nothing moved, not
a leaf quivered, the visible breaths of the dogs
rising slowly and lingering in the frosty air.
They had made short work of the snowshoe
rabbit, these dogs that were ill-tamed wolves;
and they were now drawn up in an expectant
circle. They, too, were silent, their eyes only
gleaming and their breaths drifting slowly upward. To Buck it was nothing new or strange,

this scene of old time. It was as though it had always been, the wonted way of things.

Spitz was a practised fighter. From Spitzbergen through the Arctic, and across Canada and the Barrens, he had held his own with all manner of dogs and achieved to mastery over them. Bitter rage was his, but never blind rage. In passion to rend and destroy, he never forgot that his enemy was in like passion to rend and destroy. He never rushed till he was prepared to receive a rush; never attacked till he had first defended that attack.

In vain Buck strove to sink his teeth in the neck of the big white dog. Wherever his fangs struck for the softer flesh, they were countered by the fangs of Spitz. Fang clashed fang, and lips were cut and bleeding, but Buck could not penetrate his enemy's guard. Then he warmed up and enveloped Spitz in a whirlwind of rushes. Time and time again he tried for the snow-white throat, where life bubbled near to the surface, and each time and every time Spitz slashed him and got away. Then Buck took to rushing, as though for the throat, when, suddenly drawing back his head and curving in from the side, he would drive his shoulder at the shoulder of Spitz, as a ram by which to overthrow him. But instead, Buck's shoulder was slashed down each time as Spitz leaped lightly away.

Spitz was untouched, while Buck was streaming with blood and panting hard. The fight was growing desperate. And all the while the silent and wolfish circle waited to finish off whichever dog went down. As Buck grew winded, Spitz took to rushing, and he kept him staggering for footing. Once Buck went over, and the whole circle of sixty dogs started up; but he recovered himself, almost in mid air, and the circle sank down again and waited.

But Buck possessed a quality that made for greatness—imagination. He fought by instinct, but he could fight by head as well. He rushed, as though attempting the old shoulder trick, but at the last instant swept low to the snow and in. His teeth closed on Spitz's left fore leg. There was a crunch of breaking bone, and the white dog faced him on three legs. Thrice he tried to knock him over, then repeated the trick and broke the right fore leg. Despite the pain and helplessness, Spitz struggled madly to keep up. He saw the silent circle, with gleaming eyes, lolling tongues, and silvery breaths drifting upward, closing in upon him as he had seen similar circles close in upon beaten antagonists in the past. Only this time he was the one who was beaten.

There was no hope for him. Buck was inexorable. Mercy was a thing reserved for gentler climes. He manoeuvred for the final rush. The circle had tightened till he could feel the breaths of the huskies on his flanks. He could see them, beyond Spitz and to either side, half crouching for the spring, their eyes fixed upon him. A pause seemed to fall. Every animal was motionless as though turned to stone. Only Spitz quivered and bristled as he staggered back and forth, snarling with horrible menace, as though to frighten off impending death. Then Buck sprang in and out; but while he was in, shoulder had at last squarely met shoulder. The dark circle became a dot on the moonflooded snow as Spitz disappeared from view. Buck stood and looked on, the successful champion, the dominant primordial beast who had made his kill and found it good.

THE DEATH OF LIGOUN

Blood for blood, rank for rank.
                                    —*Thlinket Code.*

"Hear now the death of Ligoun—"

The speaker ceased, or rather suspended utterance, and gazed upon me with an eye of understanding. I held the bottle between our eyes and the fire, indicated with my thumb the depth of the draught, and shoved it over to him; for was he not Palitlum, the Drinker? Many tales had he told me, and long had I waited for this scriptless scribe to speak of the things concerning Ligoun; for he, of all men living, knew these things best.

He tilted back his head with a grunt that slid swiftly into a gurgle, and the shadow of a man's torso, monstrous beneath a huge inverted bottle, wavered and danced on the frown of the cliff at our backs. Palitlum released his lips from the glass with a caressing suck and glanced regretfully up into the ghostly vault of the sky where played the wan white light of the summer borealis.

"It be strange," he said; "cold like water and hot like fire. To the drinker it giveth strength, and from the drinker it taketh away strength. It

169

maketh old men young, and young men old. To
the man who is weary it leadeth him to get up
and go onward, and to the man unweary it
burdeneth him into sleep. My brother was
possessed of the heart of a rabbit, yet did he
drink of it, and forthwith slay four of his enemies. My father was like a great wolf, showing
his teeth to all men, yet did he drink of it and
was shot through the back, running swiftly
away. It be most strange."

"It is 'Three Star,' and a better than what
they poison their bellies with down there," I
answered, sweeping my hand, as it were, over
the yawning chasm of blackness and down to
where the beach fires glinted far below—tiny
jets of flame which gave proportion and reality
to the night.

Palitlum sighed and shook his head. "Wherefore I am here with thee."

And here he embraced the bottle and me in
a look which told more eloquently than speech
of his shameless thirst.

"Nay," I said, snuggling the bottle in between my knees. "Speak now of Ligoun. Of the
'Three Star' we will hold speech hereafter."

"There be plenty, and I am not wearied," he
pleaded brazenly. "But the feel of it on my lips,
and I will speak great words of Ligoun and his
last days."

"From the drinker it taketh away strength," I
mocked, "and to the man unweary it burdeneth
him into sleep."

"Thou art wise," he rejoined, without anger
and pridelessly. "Like all of thy brothers, thou

are wise. Waking or sleeping, the 'Three Star' be with thee, yet never have I known thee to drink overlong or overmuch. And the while you gather to you the gold that hides in our mountains and the fish that swim in our seas; and Palitlum, and the brothers of Palitlum, dig the gold for thee and net the fish, and are glad to be made glad when out of thy wisdom thou deemest it fit that the 'Three Star' should wet our lips."

"I was minded to hear of Ligoun," I said impatiently. "The night grows short, and we have a sore journey to-morrow."

I yawned and made as though to rise, but Palitlum betrayed a quick anxiety, and with abruptness began:—

"It was Ligoun's desire, in his old age, that peace should be among the tribes. As a young man he had been first of the fighting men and chief over the war-chiefs of the Islands and the Passes. All his days had been full of fighting. More marks he boasted of bone and lead and iron than any other man. Three wives he had, and for each wife two sons; and the sons, eldest born and last and all died by his side in battle. Restless as the bald-face, he ranged wide and far—north to Unalaska and the Shallow Sea; south to the Queen Charlottes, ay, even did he go with the Kakes, it is told, to far Puget Sound, and slay thy brothers in their sheltered houses.

"But, as I say, in his old age he looked for peace among the tribes. Not that he was become afraid, or overfond of the corner by the fire and the well-filled pot. For he slew with the shrewdness and blood-hunger of the fiercest, drew in his belly to famine with the youngest, and with the stoutest faced the bitter seas and stinging trail. But because of his many deeds, and in punishment, a warship carried him away, even to thy country, O Hair-Face and Boston Man; and the years were many ere he came back, and I was grown to something more than a boy and something less than a young man. And Ligoun, being childless in his old age, made much of me, and grown wise, gave me of his wisdom.

" 'It be good to fight, O Palitlum,' said he. Nay, O Hair-Face, for I was unknown as Palitlum in those days, being called Olo, the Ever-Hungry. The drink was to come after. 'It be good to fight,' spake Ligoun, 'but it be foolish. In the Boston Man Country, as I saw with mine eyes, they are not given to fighting one with another, and they be strong. Wherefore, of their strength, they come against us of the Islands and Passes, and we are as camp smoke and sea mist before them. Wherefore I say it be good to fight, most good, but it be likewise foolish.'

"And because of this, though first always of the fighting men, Ligoun's voice was loudest, ever, for peace. And when he was very old, being greatest of chiefs and richest of men, he gave a potlatch. Never was there such a potlatch. Five hundred canoes were lined against the river bank, and in each canoe there came not less than ten of men and women. Eight tribes were there; from the first and oldest man to the last and youngest babe were they there. And then there were men from far-distant tribes, great travellers and seekers who had heard of the potlatch of Ligoun. And for the length of seven days they filled their bellies with his meat and drink. Eight thousand blankets did he give to them, as I well know, for who but I kept the tally and apportioned according to degree and rank? And in the end Ligoun was a poor man; but his name was on all men's lips, and other chiefs gritted their teeth in envy that he should be so great.

"And so, because there was weight to his words, he counselled peace; and he journeyed to every potlatch and feast and tribal gathering that he might counsel peace. And so it came that we journeyed together, Ligoun and I, to the great feast given by Niblack, who was chief over the river Indians of the Skoot, which is not far from the Stickeen. This was in the last days, and Ligoun was very old and very close to death. He coughed of cold weather and camp smoke, and often the red blood ran from out his mouth till we looked for him to die.

" 'Nay,' he said once at such time; 'it were better that I should die when the blood leaps to the knife, and there is a clash of steel and smell of powder, and men crying aloud what of the cold iron and quick lead.' So, it be plain, O Hair-Face, that his heart was yet strong for battle.

"It is very far from the Chilcat to the Skoot, and we were many days in the canoes. And the while the men bent to the paddles, I sat at the

feet of Ligoun and received the Law. Of small
need for me to say the Law, O Hair-Face, for it
be known to me that in this thou art well
skilled. Yet do I speak of the Law of blood for
blood, and rank for rank. Also did Ligoun go
deeper into the matter, saying:—

"'But know this, O Olo, that there be little
honor in the killing of a man less than thee. Kill
always the man who is greater, and thy honor
shall be according to his greatness. But if, of
two men, thou killest the lesser, then is shame
thine, for which the very squaws will lift their
lips at thee. As I say, peace be good; but
remember, O Olo, if kill thou must, that thou
killest by the Law.'

"It is a way of the Thlinket-folk," Palitlum
vouchsafed half apologetically.

And I remembered the gun-fighters and bad
men of my own Western land, and was not perplexed at the way of the Thlinket-folk.

"In time," Palitlum continued, "we came to
Chief Niblack and the Skoots. It was a feast
great almost as the potlatch of Ligoun. There
were we of the Chilcat, and the Sitkas, and the
Stickeens who are neighbors to the Skoots, and
the Wrangels and the Hoonahs. There were
Sundowns and Tahkos from Port Houghton,
and their neighbors the Awks from Douglass
Channel; the Naass River people, and the Tongas from north of Dixon, and the Kakes who
come from the island called Kupreanoff. Then
there were Siwashes from Vancouver, Cassiars
from the Gold Mountains, Teslin men, and
even Sticks from the Yukon Country.

"It was a mighty gathering. But first of all, there was to be a meeting of the chiefs with Niblack, and a drowning of all enmities in quass. The Russians it was who showed us the way of making quass, for so my father told me,—my father, who got it from his father before him. But to this quass had Niblack added many things, such as sugar, flour, dried apples, and hops, so that it was a man's drink, strong and good. Not so good as 'Three Star,' O Hair-Face, yet good.

"This quass-feast was for the chiefs, and the chiefs only, and there was a score of them. But Ligoun being very old and very great, it was given that I walk with him that he might lean upon my shoulder and that I might ease him down when he took his seat and raise him up when he arose. At the door of Niblack's house, which was of logs and very big, each chief, as was the custom, laid down his spear or rifle and his knife. For as thou knowest, O Hair-Face, strong drink quickens, and old hates flame up, and head and hand are swift to act. But I noted that Ligoun had brought two knives, the one he left outside the door, the other slipped under his blanket, snug to the grip. The other chiefs did likewise, and I was troubled for what was to come.

"The chiefs were ranged, sitting, in a big circle about the room. I stood at Ligoun's elbow. In the middle was the barrel of quass, and by it a slave to serve the drink. First, Niblack made oration, with much show of friendship and many fine words. Then he gave a sign, and the slave dipped a gourd full of quass and

passed it to Ligoun, as was fit, for his was the
highest rank.

"Ligoun drank it, to the last drop, and I gave
him my strength to get on his feet so that he,
too, might make oration. He had kind speech
for the many tribes, noted the greatness of Niblack to give such a feast, counselled for peace
as was his custom, and at the end said that the
quass was very good.

"Then Niblack drank, being next of rank to
Ligoun, and after him one chief and another in
degree and order. And each spoke friendly
words and said that the quass was good, till all
had drunk. Did I say all? Nay, not all, O Hair-
Face. For last of them was one, a lean and cat-
like man, young of face, with a quick and
daring eye, who drank darkly, and spat forth
upon the ground, and spoke no word.

"To not say that the quass was good were insult; to spit forth upon the ground were worse
than insult. And this very thing did he do. He
was known for a chief over the Sticks of the Yukon, and further naught was known of him.

"As I say, it was an insult. But mark this, O
Hair-Face: it was an insult, not to Niblack the
feast-giver, but to the man chiefest of rank who
sat among those of the circle. And that man
was Ligoun. There was no sound. All eyes were
upon him to see what he might do. He made no
movement. His withered lips trembled not into
speech; nor did a nostril quiver, nor an eyelid
droop. But I saw that he looked wan and gray,
as I have seen old men look of bitter mornings
when famine pressed, and the women wailed

and the children whimpered, and there was no meat nor sign of meat. And as the old men looked, so looked Ligoun.

"There was no sound. It were as a circle of the dead, but that each chief felt beneath his blanket to make sure, and that each chief glanced to his neighbor, right and left, with a measuring eye. I was a stripling; the things I had seen were few; yet I knew it to be the moment one meets but once in all a lifetime.

"The Stick rose up, with every eye upon him, and crossed the room till he stood before Ligoun.

" 'I am Opitsah, the Knife,' he said.

"But Ligoun said naught, nor looked at him, but gazed unblinking at the ground.

" 'You are Ligoun,' Opitsah said. 'You have killed many men. I am still alive.'

"And still Ligoun said naught, though he made the sign to me and with my strength arose and stood upright on his two feet. He was as an old pine, naked and gray, but still a-shoulder to the frost and storm. His eyes were unblinking, and as he had not heard Opitsah, so it seemed he did not see him.

"And Opitsah was mad with anger, and danced stiff-legged before him, as men do when they wish to give another shame. And Opitsah sang a song of his own greatness and the greatness of his people, filled with bad words for the Chilcats and for Ligoun. And as he danced and sang, Opitsah threw off his blanket and with his knife drew bright circles before

the face of Ligoun. And the song he sang was
the Song of the Knife.

"And there was no other sound, only the
singing of Opitsah, and the circle of chiefs that
were as dead, save that the flash of the knife
seemed to draw smouldering fire from their
eyes. And Ligoun, also, was very still. Yet did
he know his death, and was unafraid. And the
knife sang closer and yet closer to his face, but
his eyes were unblinking and he swayed not to
right or left, or this way or that.

"And Opitsah drove in the knife, so, twice on
the forehead of Ligoun, and the red blood
leaped after it. And then it was that Ligoun
gave me the sign to bear up under him with my
youth that he might walk. And he laughed with
a great scorn, full in the face of Opitsah, the
Knife. And he brushed Opitsah to the side, as
one brushes to the side a low-hanging branch
on the trail and passes on.

"And I knew and understood, for there was
but shame in the killing of Opitsah before the
faces of a score of greater chiefs. I remembered
the Law, and knew Ligoun had it in mind to
kill by the Law. And who, chiefest of rank but
himself, was there but Niblack? And toward
Niblack, leaning on my arm, he walked. And to
his other arm, clinging and striking, was Opitsah, too small to soil with his blood the hands
of so great a man. And though the knife of Opitsah bit in again and again, Ligoun noted it
not, nor winced. And in this fashion we three
went our way across the room, Niblack sitting
in his blanket and fearful of our coming.

"And now old hates flamed up and forgotten grudges were remembered. Lamuk, a Kake, had had a brother drowned in the bad water of the Stickeen, and the Stickeens had not paid in blankets for their bad water, as was the custom to pay. So Lamuk drove straight with his long knife to the heart of Klok-Kutz the Stickeen. And Katchahook remembered a quarrel of the Naass River people with the Tongas of north of Dixon, and the chief of the Tongas he slew with a pistol which made much noise. And the blood-hunger gripped all the men who sat in the circle, and chief slew chief, or was slain, as chance might be. Also did they stab and shoot at Ligoun, for whoso killed him won great honor and would be unforgotten for the deed. And they were about him like wolves about a moose, only they were so many they were in their own way, and they slew one another to make room. And there was great confusion.

"But Ligoun went slowly, without haste, as though many years were yet before him. It seemed that he was certain he would make his kill, in his own way, ere they could slay him. And as I say, he went slowly, and knives bit into him, and he was red with blood. And though none sought after me, who was a mere stripling, yet did the knives find me, and the hot bullets burn me. And still Ligoun leaned his weight on my youth, and Opitsah struck at him, and we three went forward. And when we stood by Niblack, he was afraid, and covered his head with his blanket. The Skoots were ever cowards.

"And Goolzug and Kadishan, the one a fish-eater and the other a meat-killer, closed together for the honor of their tribes. And they raged madly about, and in their battling swung against the knees of Opitsah, who was over-thrown and trampled upon. And a knife, sing-ing through the air, smote Skulpin, of the Sitkas, in the throat, and he flung his arms out blindly, reeling, and dragged me down in his fall.

"And from the ground I beheld Ligoun bend over Niblack, and uncover the blanket from his head, and turn up his face to the light. And Li-goun was in no haste. Being blinded with his own blood, he swept it out of his eyes with the back of his hand, so he might see and be sure. And when he was sure that the upturned face was the face of Niblack, he drew the knife across his throat as one draws a knife across the throat of a trembling deer. And then Ligoun stood erect, singing his death-song and swaying gently to and fro. And Skulpin, who had dragged me down, shot with a pistol from where he lay, and Ligoun toppled and fell, as an old pine topples and falls in the teeth of the wind."

Palitlum ceased. His eyes, smouldering moodily, were bent upon the fire, and his cheek was dark with blood.

"And thou, Palitlum?" I demanded. "And thou?"

"I? I did remember the Law, and I slew Opitsah the Knife, which was well. And I drew Ligoun's own knife from the throat of Niblack, and slew Skulpin, who had dragged me down. For I was a stripling, and I could slay any man and it were honor. And further, Ligoun being dead, there was no need for my youth, and I laid about me with his knife, choosing the chiefest of rank that yet remained."

Palitlum fumbled under his shirt and drew forth a beaded sheath, and from the sheath, a knife. It was a knife home-wrought and crudely fashioned from a whip-saw file; a knife such as one may find possessed by old men in a hundred Alaskan villages.

"The knife of Ligoun?" I said, and Palitlum nodded.

"And for the knife of Ligoun," I said, "will I give thee ten bottles of 'Three Star.'"

But Palitlum looked at me slowly. "Hair-Face, I am weak as water, and easy as a woman. I have soiled my belly with quass, and hooch, and 'Three Star.' My eyes are blunted, my ears have lost their keenness, and my strength has gone into fat. And I am without honor in these days, and am called Palitlum, the Drinker. Yet honor was mine at the pot-latch of Niblack, on the Skoot, and the memory of it, and the memory of Ligoun, be dear to me. Nay, didst thou turn the sea itself into 'Three Star' and say that it were all mine for the knife, yet would I keep the knife. I am Palitlum, the Drinker, but I was once Olo, the Ever-Hungry, who bore up Ligoun with his youth!"

"Thou art a great man, Palitlum," I said, "and I honor thee."

Palitlum reached out his hand.

"The 'Three Star' between thy knees be mine for the tale I have told," he said.

And as I looked on the frown of the cliff at our backs, I saw the shadow of a man's torso, monstrous beneath a huge inverted bottle.

KEESH, THE SON
OF KEESH

"Thus will I give six blankets, warm and double; six files, large and hard; six Hudson Bay knives, keen-edged and long; two canoes, the work of Mogum, The Maker of Things; ten dogs, heavy-shouldered and strong in the harness; and three guns—the trigger of one be broken, but it is a good gun and can doubtless be mended."

Keesh paused and swept his eyes over the circle of intent faces. It was the time of the Great Fishing, and he was bidding to Gnob for Su-Su his daughter. The place was the St. George Mission by the Yukon, and the tribes had gathered for many a hundred miles. From north, south, east, and west they had come, even from Tozikakat and far Tana-naw.

"And further, O Gnob, thou art chief of the Tana-naw; and I, Keesh, the son of Keesh, am chief of the Thlunget. Wherefore, when my seed springs from the loins of thy daughter, there shall be a friendship between the tribes, a great friendship, and Tana-naw and Thlunget shall be brothers of the blood in the time to come. What I have said I will do, that will I do. And how is it with you, O Gnob, in this matter?"

Gnob nodded his head gravely, his gnarled and age-twisted face inscrutably masking the soul that dwelt behind. His narrow eyes burned like twin coals through their narrow slits, as he piped in a high-cracked voice, "But that is not all."

"What more?" Keesh demanded. "Have I not offered full measure? Was there ever yet a Tana-naw maiden who fetched so great a price? Then name her!"

An open snicker passed round the circle, and Keesh knew that he stood in shame before these people.

"Nay, nay, good Keesh, thou dost not understand." Gnob made a soft, stroking gesture. "The price is fair. It is a good price. Nor do I question the broken trigger. But that is not all. What of the man?"

"Ay, what of the man?" the circle snarled.

"It is said," Gnob's shrill voice piped, "it is said that Keesh does not walk in the way of his fathers. It is said that he has wandered into the dark, after strange gods, and that he is become afraid."

The face of Keesh went dark. "It is a lie!" he thundered. "Keesh is afraid of no man!"

"It is said," old Gnob piped on, "that he has harkened to the speech of the white man up at the Big House, and that he bends head to the white man's god, and, moreover, that blood is displeasing to the white man's god."

Keesh dropped his eyes, and his hands clenched passionately. The savage circle laughed derisively, and in the ear of Gnob whispered Madwan, the shaman, high-priest of the tribe and maker of medicine.

The shaman poked among the shadows on the rim of the firelight and roused up a slender young boy, whom he brought face to face with Keesh; and in the hand of Keesh he thrust a knife.

Gnob leaned forward. "Keesh! O Keesh! Darest thou to kill a man? Behold! This be Kitz-noo, a slave. Strike, O Keesh, strike with the strength of thy arm!"

The boy trembled and waited the stroke. Keesh looked at him, and thoughts of Mr. Brown's higher morality floated through his mind, and strong upon him was a vision of the leaping flames of Mr. Brown's particular brand of hell-fire. The knife fell to the ground, and the boy sighed and went out beyond the firelight with shaking knees. At the feet of Gnob sprawled a wolf-dog, which bared its gleaming teeth and prepared to spring after the boy. But the shaman ground his foot into the brute's body, and so doing, gave Gnob an idea.

"And then, O Keesh, what wouldst thou do, should a man do this thing to you?"—as he spoke, Gnob held a ribbon of salmon to White Fang, and when the animal attempted to take it, smote him sharply on the nose with a stick. "And afterward, O Keesh, wouldst thou do thus?"—White Fang was cringing back on his belly and fawning to the hand of Gnob.

"Listen!"—leaning on the arm of Madwan, Gnob had risen to his feet. "I am very old, and because I am very old I will tell thee things. Thy father, Keesh, was a mighty man. And he did love the song of the bowstring in battle, and these eyes have beheld him cast a spear till the head stood out beyond a man's body. But thou art unlike. Since thou left the Raven to worship the Wolf, thou art become afraid of blood, and thou makest thy people afraid. This is not good. For behold, when I was a boy, even as Kitz-noo there, there was no white man in all the land. But they came, one by one, these white men, till now they are many. And they are a restless breed, never content to rest by the fire with a full belly and let the morrow bring its own meat. A curse was laid upon them, it would seem, and they must work it out in toil and hardship."

Keesh was startled. A recollection of a hazy story told by Mr. Brown of one Adam, of old time, came to him, and it seemed that Mr. Brown had spoken true.

"So they lay hands upon all they behold, these white men, and they go everywhere and behold all things. And ever do more follow in their steps, so that if nothing be done they will come to possess all the land and there will be no room for the tribes of the Raven. Wherefore it is meet that we fight with them till none are left. Then will we hold the passes and the land, and perhaps our children and our children's children shall flourish and grow fat. There is a great struggle to come, when Wolf and Raven shall grapple; but Keesh will not fight, nor will he let his people fight. So it is not well that he should take to him my daughter. Thus have I spoken, I, Gnob, chief of the Tana-naw."

"But the white men are good and great," Keesh made answer. "The white men have taught us many things. The white men have given us blankets and knives and guns, such as we have never made and never could make. I remember in what manner we lived before they came. I was unborn then, but I have it from my father. When we went on the hunt we must creep so close to the moose that a spear-cast would cover the distance. To-day we use the white man's rifle, and farther away than can a child's cry be heard. We ate fish and meat and berries—there was nothing else to eat—and we ate without salt. How many be there among you who care to go back to the fish and meat without salt?"

It would have sunk home, had not Madwan leaped to his feet ere silence could come. "And first a question to thee, Keesh. The white man up at the Big House tells you that it is wrong to kill. Yet do we not know that the white men kill? Have we forgotten the great fight on the Koyokuk? or the great fight at Nuklukyeto, where three white men killed twenty of the Tozikakats? Do you think we no longer remember the three men of the Tana-naw that the white man Macklewrath killed? Tell me, O Keesh,

why does the Shaman Brown teach you that it
is wrong to fight, when all his brothers fight?"

"Nay, nay, there is no need to answer," Gnob
piped, while Keesh struggled with the paradox.
"It is very simple. The Good Man Brown would
hold the Raven tight whilst his brothers pluck
the feathers." He raised his voice. "But so long
as there is one Tana-naw to strike a blow, or
one maiden to bear a man-child, the Raven
shall not be plucked!"

Gnob turned to a husky young man across
the fire. "And what sayest thou, Makamuk, who
art brother to Su-Su?"

Makamuk came to his feet. A long face-scar
lifted his upper lip into a perpetual grin which
belied the glowing ferocity of his eyes. "This
day," he began with cunning irrelevance, "I
came by the Trader Macklewrath's cabin. And
in the door I saw a child laughing at the sun.
And the child looked at me with the Trader
Macklewrath's eyes, and it was frightened. The
mother ran to it and quieted it. The mother
was Ziska, the Thlunget woman."

A snarl of rage rose up and drowned his
voice, which he stilled by turning dramatically
upon Keesh with outstretched arm and ac-
cusing finger.

"So? You give your women away, you Thlunget, and come to the Tana-naw for more? But
we have need of our women, Keesh; for we
must breed men, many men, against the day
when the Raven grapples with the Wolf."

Through the storm of applause, Gnob's voice

shrilled clear. "And thou, Nossabok, who art her favorite brother?"

The young fellow was slender and graceful, with the strong aquiline nose and high brows of his type; but from some nervous affliction the lid of one eye drooped at odd times in a suggestive wink. Even as he arose it so drooped and rested a moment against his cheek. But it was not greeted with the accustomed laughter. Every face was grave. "I, too, passed by the Trader Macklewrath's cabin," he rippled in soft, girlish tones, wherein there was much of youth and much of his sister. "And I saw Indians with the sweat running into their eyes and their knees shaking with weariness—I say, I saw Indians groaning under the logs for the store which the Trader Macklewrath is to build. And with my eyes I saw them chopping wood to keep the Shaman Brown's Big House warm through the frost of the long nights. This be squaw work. Never shall the Tana-naw do the like. We shall be blood brothers to men, not squaws: and the Thlunget be squaws."

A deep silence fell, and all eyes centred on Keesh. He looked about him carefully, deliberately, full into the face of each grown man. "So," he said passionlessly. And "So," he repeated. Then turned on his heel without further word and passed out into the darkness.

Wading among sprawling babies and bristling wolf-dogs, he threaded the great camp, and on its outskirts came upon a woman at work by the light of a fire. With strings of bark stripped from the long roots of creeping vines, she was braiding rope for the Fishing. For some time, without speech, he watched her deft hands bringing law and order out of the unruly mass of curling fibres. She was good to look upon, swaying there to her task, strong-limbed, deep-chested, and with hips made for mother-hood. And the bronze of her face was golden in the flickering light, her hair blue-black, her eyes jet.

"O Su-Su," he spoke finally, "thou hast looked upon me kindly in the days that have gone and in the days yet young—"

"I looked kindly upon thee for that thou wert chief of the Thlunget," she answered quickly, "and because thou wert big and strong."

"Ay—"

"But that was in the old days of the Fishing," she hastened to add, "before the Shaman Brown came and taught thee ill things and led thy feet on strange trails."

"But I would tell thee the—"

She held up one hand in a gesture which reminded him of her father. "Nay, I know already the speech that stirs in thy throat, O Keesh, and I make answer now. It so happeneth that the fish of the water and the beasts of the forest bring forth after their kind. And this is good. Likewise it happeneth to women. It is for them to bring forth their kind, and even the maiden, while she is yet a maiden, feels the pang of the birth, and the pain of the breast, and the small hands at the neck. And when such feeling is strong, then does each maiden look about her with secret eyes for the man—for

the man who shall be fit to father her kind. So
have I felt. So did I feel when I looked upon
thee and found thee big and strong, a hunter
and fighter of beasts and men, well able to win
meat when I should eat for two, well able to
keep danger afar off when my helplessness
drew nigh. But that was before the day the
Shaman Brown came into the land and taught
thee—"

"But it is not right, Su-Su. I have it on good
word—"

"It is not right to kill. I know what thou
wouldst say. Then breed thou after thy kind,
the kind that does not kill; but come not on
such quest among the Tana-naw. For it is said
in the time to come, that the Raven shall
grapple with the Wolf. I do not know, for this
be the affair of men; but I do know that it is for
me to bring forth men against that time."

"Su-Su," Keesh broke in, "thou must hear
me—"

"A *man* would beat me with a stick and
make me hear," she sneered. "But thou . . .
here!" She thrust a bunch of bark into his hand.
"I cannot give thee myself, but this, yes. It
looks fittest in thy hands. It is squaw work, so
braid away."

He flung it from him, the angry blood pounding a muddy path under his bronze.

"One thing more," she went on. "There be an
old custom which thy father and mine were not
strangers to. When a man falls in battle, his
scalp is carried away in token. Very good. But
thou, who have forsworn the Raven, must do

more. Thou must bring me, not scalps, but
heads, two heads, and then will I give thee, not
bark, but a brave-beaded belt, and sheath, and
long Russian knife. Then will I look kindly
upon thee once again, and all will be well."

"So," the man pondered. "So." Then he
turned and passed out through the light.

"Nay, O Keesh!" she called after him. "Not
two heads, but three at least!"

But Keesh remained true to his conversion,
lived uprightly, and made his tribespeople obey
the gospel as propounded by the Rev. Jackson
Brown. Through all the time of the Fishing he
gave no heed to the Tana-naw, nor took notice
of the sly things which were said, nor of the
laughter of the women of the many tribes. After the Fishing, Gnob and his people, with
great store of salmon, sun-dried and smoke-
cured, departed for the Hunting on the head
reaches of the Tana-naw. Keesh watched them
go, but did not fail in his attendance at Mission
service, where he prayed regularly and led the
singing with his deep bass voice.

The Rev. Jackson Brown delighted in that
deep bass voice, and because of his sterling
qualities deemed him the most promising convert. Macklewrath doubted this. He did not believe in the efficacy of the conversion of the
heathen, and he was not slow in speaking his
mind. But Mr. Brown was a large man, in his
way, and he argued it out with such convin-
cingness, all of one long fall night, that the
trader, driven from position after position, fi-

nally announced in desperation, "Knock out my brains with apples, Brown, if I don't become a convert myself, if Keesh holds fast, true blue, for two years!" Mr. Brown never lost an opportunity, so he clinched the matter on the spot with a virile hand-grip, and thenceforth the conduct of Keesh was to determine the ultimate abiding-place of Macklewrath's soul.

But there came news one day, after the winter's rime had settled down over the land sufficiently for travel. A Tana-naw man arrived at the St. George Mission in quest of ammunition and bringing information that Su-Su had set eyes on Nee-Koo, a nervy young hunter who had bid brilliantly for her by old Gnob's fire. It was at about this time that the Rev. Jackson Brown came upon Keesh by the wood-trail which leads down to the river. Keesh had his best dogs in the harness, and shoved under the sled-lashings was his largest and finest pair of snow-shoes.

"Where goest thou, O Keesh? Hunting?" Mr. Brown asked, falling into the Indian manner.

Keesh looked him steadily in the eyes for a full minute, then started up his dogs. Then again, turning his deliberate gaze upon the missionary, he answered, "No; I go to hell."

In an open space, striving to burrow into the snow as though for shelter from the appalling desolateness, huddled three dreary lodges. Ringed all about, a dozen paces away, was the sombre forest. Overhead there was no keen, blue sky of naked space, but a vague, misty

curtain, pregnant with snow, which had drawn
between. There was no wind, no sound, nothing but the snow and silence. Nor was there
even the general stir of life about the camp; for
the hunting party had run upon the flank of the
caribou herd and the kill had been large. Thus,
after the period of fasting had come the pleni-
tude of feasting, and thus, in broad daylight,
they slept heavily under their roofs of moosehide.

By a fire, before one of the lodges, five pairs
of snow-shoes stood on end in their element,
and by the fire sat Su-Su. The hood of her
squirrel-skin parka was about her hair, and
well drawn up around her throat; but her
hands were unmittened and nimbly at work
with needle and sinew, completing the last fantastic design on a belt of leather faced with
bright scarlet cloth. A dog, somewhere at the
rear of one of the lodges, raised a short, sharp
bark, then ceased as abruptly as it had begun.
Once, her father, in the lodge at her back,
gurgled and grunted in his sleep. "Bad
dreams," she smiled to herself. "He grows old,
and that last joint was too much."

She placed the last bead, knotted the sinew,
and replenished the fire. Then, after gazing
long into the flames, she lifted her head to the
harsh *crunch-crunch* of a moccasined foot
against the flinty snow granules. Keesh was at
her side, bending slightly forward to a load
which he bore upon his back. This was
wrapped loosely in a soft-tanned moosehide,
and he dropped it carelessly into the snow and

sat down. They looked at each other long and without speech.

"It is a far fetch, O Keesh," she said at last, "a far fetch from St. George Mission by the Yukon."

"Ay," he made answer, absently, his eyes fixed keenly upon the belt and taking note of its girth. "But where is the knife?" he demanded.

"Here." She drew it from inside her parka and flashed its naked length in the firelight. "It is a good knife."

"Give it me!" he commanded.

"Nay, O Keesh," she laughed. "It may be that thou wast not born to wear it."

"Give it me!" he reiterated, without change of tone. "I was so born."

But her eyes, glancing coquettishly past him to the moosehide, saw the snow about it slowly reddening. "It is blood, Keesh?" she asked.

"Ay, it is blood. But give me the belt and the long Russian knife."

She felt suddenly afraid, but thrilled when he took the belt roughly from her, thrilled to the roughness. She looked at him softly, and was aware of a pain at the breast and of small hands clutching her throat.

"It was made for a smaller man," he remarked grimly, drawing in his abdomen and clasping the buckle at the first hole.

Su-Su smiled, and her eyes were yet softer. Again she felt the soft hands at her throat. He was good to look upon, and the belt was indeed small, made for a smaller man; but what did it matter? She could make many belts.

"But the blood?" she asked, urged on by a
hope new-born and growing. "The blood,
Keesh? Is it ... are they ... heads?"

"Ay."

"They must be very fresh, else would the
blood be frozen."

"Ay, it is not cold, and they be fresh, quite
fresh."

"Oh, Keesh!" Her face was warm and bright.
"And for me?"

"Ay; for thee."

He took hold of a corner of the hide, flirted it
open, and rolled the heads out before her.

"Three," he whispered savagely; "nay, four at
least."

But she sat transfixed. There they lay—the
soft-featured Nee-Koo; the gnarled old face of
Gnob; Makamuk, grinning at her with his lifted
upper lip; and lastly, Nossabok, his eyelid, up
to its old trick, dropped on his girlish cheek in
a suggestive wink. There they lay, the firelight
flashing upon and playing over them, and from
each of them a widening circle dyed the snow
to scarlet.

Thawed by the fire, the white crust gave way
beneath the head of Gnob, which rolled over
like a thing alive, spun around, and came to
rest at her feet. But she did not move. Keesh,
too, sat motionless, his eyes unblinking, centred
steadfastly upon her.

Once, in the forest, an overburdened pine
dropped its load of snow, and the echoes rever-
berated hollowly down the gorge; but neither
stirred. The short day had been waning fast,

and darkness was wrapping round the camp when White Fang trotted up toward the fire. He paused to reconnoitre, but not being driven back, came closer. His nose shot swiftly to the side, nostrils a-tremble and bristles rising along the spine; and straight and true, he followed the sudden scent to his master's head. He sniffed it gingerly at first and licked the forehead with his red lolling tongue. Then he sat abruptly down, pointed his nose up at the first faint star, and raised the long wolf-howl.

This brought Su-Su to herself. She glanced across at Keesh, who had unsheathed the Russian knife and was watching her intently. His face was firm and set, and in it she read the law. Slipping back the hood of her parka, she bared her neck and rose to her feet. There she paused and took a long look about her, at the rimming forest, at the faint stars in the sky, at the camp, at the snow-shoes in the snow—a last long comprehensive look at life. A light breeze stirred her hair from the side, and for the space of one deep breath she turned her head and followed it around until she met it full-faced.

Then she thought of her children, ever to be unborn, and she walked over to Keesh and said, "I am ready."

IN THE FORESTS
OF THE NORTH

A weary journey beyond the last scrub timber and straggling copses, into the heart of the
Barrens where the niggard North is supposed
to deny the Earth, are to be found great sweeps
of forests and stretches of smiling land. But this
the world is just beginning to know. The
world's explorers have known it, from time to
time, but hitherto they have never returned to
tell the world.

The Barrens—well, they are the Barrens, the
bad lands of the Arctic, the deserts of the
Circle, the bleak and bitter home of the musk-
ox and the lean plains wolf. So Avery Van
Brunt found them, treeless and cheerless,
sparsely clothed with moss and lichens, and al-
together uninviting. At least so he found them
till he penetrated to the white blank spaces on
the map, and came upon undreamed-of rich
spruce forests and unrecorded Eskimo tribes. It
had been his intention, (and his bid for fame),
to break up these white blank spaces and diver-
sify them with the black markings of moun-

tain-chains, sinks and basins, and sinuous river
courses; and it was with added delight that he
came to speculate upon the possibilities of timber belts and native villages.

Avery Van Brunt, or, in full distinction, Pro-
fessor A. Van Brunt of the Geological Survey,
was second in command of the expedition, and
first in command of the sub-expedition which
he had led on a side tour of some half a thousand miles up one of the branches of the Thelon
and which he was now leading into one of his
unrecorded villages. At his back plodded eight
men, two of them French-Canadian *voyageurs*,
and the remainder strapping Crees from Mani-
toba-way. He, alone, was full-blooded Saxon,
and his blood was pounding fiercely through
his veins to the traditions of his race. Clive and
Hastings, Drake and Raleigh, Hengest and
Horsa, walked with him. First of all men of his
breed was he to enter this lone Northland village, and at the thought an exultancy came
upon him, an exaltation, and his followers
noted that his leg-weariness fell from him and
that he insensibly quickened the pace.

The village emptied itself, and a motley
crowd trooped out to meet him, men in the
forefront, with bows and spears clutched menacingly, and women and children faltering
timidly in the rear. Van Brunt lifted his right
arm and made the universal peace sign, a sign
which all peoples know, and the villagers answered in peace. But to his chagrin, a skin-clad
man ran forward and thrust out his hand with
a familiar "Hello." He was a bearded man, with

cheeks and brow bronzed to copper-brown, and in him Van Brunt knew his kind.

"Who are you?" he asked, gripping the extended hand. "Andrée?"

"Who's Andrée?" the man asked back.

Van Brunt looked at him more sharply. "By George, you've been here some time."

"Five years," the man answered, a dim flicker of pride in his eyes. "But come on, let's talk."

"Let them camp alongside of me," he answered Van Brunt's glance at his party. "Old Tantlatch will take care of them. Come on."

He swung off in a long stride, Van Brunt following at his heels through the village. In irregular fashion, wherever the ground favored, the lodges of moose hide were pitched. Van Brunt ran his practised eye over them and calculated.

"Two hundred, not counting the young ones," he summed up.

The man nodded. "Pretty close to it. But here's where I live, out of the thick of it, you know—more privacy and all that. Sit down. I'll eat with you when your men get something cooked up. I've forgotten what tea tastes like. . . . Five years and never a taste or smell. . . . Any tobacco? . . . A-h, thanks, and a pipe? Good. Now for a firestick and we'll see if the weed has lost its cunning."

He scratched the match with the painstaking care of the woodsman, cherished its young flame as though there were never another in all the world, and drew in the first mouthful of smoke. This he retained meditatively for a time, and blew out through his pursed lips slowly

and caressingly. Then his face seemed to soften
as he leaned back, and a soft blur to film his
eyes. He sighed heavily, happily, with immeasurable content, and then said suddenly:

"God! But that tastes good!"

Van Brunt nodded sympathetically. "Five
years, you say?"

"Five years." The man sighed again. "And
you, I presume, wish to know about it, being
naturally curious, and this a sufficiently strange
situation, and all that. But it's not much. I
came in from Edmonton after musk-ox, and like
Pike and the rest of them, had my mischances,
only I lost my party and outfit. Starvation,
hardship, the regular tale, you know, sole sur-
vivor and all that, till I crawled into Tantlatch's, here, on hand and knee."

"Five years," Van Brunt murmured retro-
spectively, as though turning things over in his
mind.

"Five years on February last. I crossed the
Great Slave early in May—"

"And you are . . . Fairfax?" Van Brunt in-
terjected.

The man nodded.

"Let me see . . . John, I think it is, John Fairfax."

"How did you know?" Fairfax queried lazily,
half-absorbed in curling smoke-spirals upward
in the quiet air.

"The papers were full of it at the time. Prevanche—"

"Prevanche!" Fairfax sat up, suddenly alert.
"He was lost in the Smoke Mountains."

"Yes, but he pulled through and came out."

Fairfax settled back again and resumed his smoke-spirals. "I am glad to hear it," he remarked reflectively. "Prevanche was a bully fellow if he *did* have ideas about head-straps, the beggar. And he pulled through? Well, I'm glad."

Five years . . . the phrase drifted recurrently through Van Brunt's thought, and somehow the face of Emily Southwaithe seemed to rise up and take form before him. Five years . . . A wedge of wild-fowl honked low overhead and at sight of the encampment veered swiftly to the north into the smouldering sun. Van Brunt could not follow them. He pulled out his watch. It was an hour past midnight. The northward clouds flushed bloodily, and rays of sombre-red shot southward, firing the gloomy woods with a lurid radiance. The air was in breathless calm, not a needle quivered, and the least sounds of the camp were distinct and clear as trumpet calls. The Crees and *voyageurs* felt the spirit of it and mumbled in dreamy undertones, and the cook unconsciously subdued the clatter of pot and pan. Somewhere a child was crying, and from the depths of the forest, like a silver thread, rose a woman's voice in mournful chant: "O-o-o-o-o-o-a-haa-ha-a-ha-aa-a-a, O-o-o-o-o-o-a-ha-a-ha-a."

Van Brunt shivered and rubbed the backs of his hands briskly.

"And they gave me up for dead?" his companion asked slowly.

"Well, you never came back, so your friends—"

"Promptly forgot." Fairfax laughed harshly, defiantly.

"Why didn't you come out?"

"Partly disinclination, I suppose, and partly because of circumstances over which I had no control. You see, Tantlatch, here, was down with a broken leg when I made his acquaintance,—a nasty fracture,—and I set it for him and got him into shape. I stayed some time, getting my strength back. I was the first white man he had seen, and of course I seemed very wise and showed his people no end of things. Coached them up in military tactics, among other things, so that they conquered the four other tribal villages, (which you have not yet seen), and came to rule the land. And they naturally grew to think a good deal of me, so much so that when I was ready to go they wouldn't hear of it. Were most hospitable, in fact. Put a couple of guards over me and watched me day and night. And then Tantlatch offered me inducements,—in a sense, inducements,—so to say, and as it didn't matter much one way or the other, I reconciled myself to remaining."

"I knew your brother at Freiburg. I am Van Brunt."

Fairfax reached forward impulsively and shook his hand. "You were Billy's friend, eh? Poor Billy! He spoke of you often."

"Rum meeting place, though," he added, casting an embracing glance over the primordial landscape and listening for a moment to the woman's mournful notes. "Her man was clawed by a bear, and she's taking it hard."

"Beastly life!" Van Brunt grimaced his disgust. "I suppose, after five years of it, civilization will be sweet? What do you say?"

Fairfax's face took on a stolid expression. "Oh, I don't know. At least they're honest folk and live according to their lights. And then they are amazingly simple. No complexity about them, no thousand and one subtle ramifications to every single emotion they experience. They love, fear, hate, are angered, or made happy, in common, ordinary, and unmistakable terms. It may be a beastly life, but at least it is easy to live. No philandering, no dallying. If a woman likes you, she'll not be backward in telling you so. If she hates you, she'll tell you so, and then, if you feel inclined, you can beat her, but the thing is, she knows precisely what you mean, and you know precisely what she means. No mistakes, no misunderstandings. It has its charm, after civilization's fitful fever. Comprehend?"

"No, it's a pretty good life," he continued, after a pause; "good enough for me, and I intend to stay with it."

Van Brunt lowered his head in a musing manner, and an imperceptible smile played on his mouth. No philandering, no dallying, no misunderstanding. Fairfax also was taking it hard, he thought, just because Emily Southwaithe had been mistakenly clawed by a bear.

And not a bad sort of a bear, either, was Carlton Southwaithe.

"But you are coming along with me," Van Brunt said deliberately.

"No, I'm not."

"Yes, you are."

"Life's too easy here, I tell you." Fairfax spoke with decision. "I understand everything, and I am understood. Summer and winter alternate like the sun flashing through the palings of a fence, the seasons are a blur of light and shade, and time slips by, and life slips by, and then . . . a wailing in the forest, and the dark. Listen!"

He held up his hand, and the silver thread of the woman's sorrow rose through the silence and the calm. Fairfax joined in softly.

"O-o-o-o-o-o-a-haaa-ha-a-ha-aa-a-a, O-o-o-o-o-o-a-ha-a-ha-a," he sang. "Can't you hear it? Can't you see it? The women mourning? the funeral chant? my hair white-locked and patriarchal? my skins wrapped in rude splendor about me? my hunting-spear by my side? And who shall say it is not well?"

Van Brunt looked at him coolly. "Fairfax, you are a damned fool. Five years of this is enough to knock any man, and you are in an unhealthy, morbid condition. Further, Carlton Southwaithe is dead."

Van Brunt filled his pipe and lighted it, the while watching slyly and with almost professional interest. Fairfax's eyes flashed on the instant, his fists clenched, he half rose up, then his muscles relaxed and he seeemed to brood.

Michael, the cook, signalled that the meal was ready, but Van Brunt motioned back to delay. The silence hung heavy, and he fell to analyzing the forest scents, the odors of mould and rotting vegetation, the resiny smells of pine cones and needles, the aromatic savors of many camp-smokes. Twice Fairfax looked up, but said nothing, and then:

"And ... Emily...?"

"Three years a widow; still a widow."

Another long silence settled down, to be broken by Fairfax finally with a naïve smile. "I guess you're right, Van Brunt. I'll go along."

"I knew you would." Van Brunt laid his hand on Fairfax's shoulder. "Of course, one cannot know, but I imagine—for one in her position— she has had offers—"

"When do you start?" Fairfax interrupted.

"After the men have had some sleep. Which reminds me, Michael is getting angry, so come and eat."

After supper, when the Crees and *voyageurs* had rolled into their blankets, snoring, the two men lingered by the dying fire. There was much to talk about,—wars and politics and explorations, the doings of men and the happening of things, mutual friends, marriages, deaths,—five years of history for which Fairfax clamored.

"So the Spanish fleet was bottled up in Santiago," Van Brunt was saying, when a young woman stepped lightly before him and stood by Fairfax's side. She looked swiftly into his

face, then turned a troubled gaze upon Van
Brunt.

"Chief Tantlatch's daughter, sort of
princess," Fairfax explained, with an honest
flush. "One of the inducements, in short, to
make me stay. Thom, this is Van Brunt, friend
of mine."

Van Brunt held out his hand, but the woman
maintained a rigid repose quite in keeping with
her general appearance. Not a line of her face
softened, not a feature unbent. She looked him
straight in the eyes, her own piercing, question-
ing, searching.

"Precious lot she understands," Fairfax
laughed. "Her first introduction, you know. But
as you were saying, with the Spanish fleet
bottled up in Santiago?"

Thom crouched down by her husband's side,
motionless as a bronze statue, only her eyes
flashing from face to face in ceaseless search.
And Avery Van Brunt, as he talked on and on,
felt a nervousness under the dumb gaze. In the
midst of his most graphic battle descriptions,
he would become suddenly conscious of the
black eyes burning into him, and would
stumble and flounder till he could catch the
gait and go again. Fairfax, hands clasped
round knees, pipe out, absorbed, spurred him
on when he lagged, and repictured the world he
thought he had forgotten.

One hour passed, and two, and Fairfax rose
reluctantly to his feet. "And Cronje was cornered, eh? Well, just wait a moment till I run
over to Tantlatch. He'll be expecting you, and

I'll arrange for you to see him after breakfast.
That will be all right, won't it?"

He went off between the pines, and Van
Brunt found himself staring into Thom's warm
eyes. Five years, he mused, and she can't be
more than twenty now. A most remarkable
creature. Being Eskimo, she should have a little
flat excuse for a nose, and lo, it is neither broad
nor flat, but aquiline, with nostrils delicately
and sensitively formed as any fine lady's of a
whiter breed—the Indian strain somewhere, be
assured, Avery Van Brunt. And, Avery Van
Brunt, don't be nervous, she won't eat you;
she's only a woman, and not a bad-looking one
at that. Oriental rather than aborigine. Eyes
large and fairly wide apart, with just the faintest hint of Mongol obliquity. Thom, you're an
anomaly. You're out of place here among these
Eskimos, even if your father is one. Where did
your mother come from? or your grandmother?
And Thom, my dear, you're a beauty, a frigid,
frozen little beauty with Alaskan lava in your
blood, and please don't look at me that way.

He laughed and stood up. Her insistent stare
disconcerted him. A dog was prowling among
the grub-sacks. He would drive it away and
place them into safety against Fairfax's return.
But Thom stretched out a detaining hand and
stood up, facing him.

"You?" she said, in the Arctic tongue which
differs little from Greenland to Point Barrow.
"You?"

And the swift expression of her face demanded all for which "you" stood, his reason

for existence, his presence there, his relation to
her husband—everything.

"Brother," he answered in the same tongue,
with a sweeping gesture to the south. "Brothers
we be, your man and I."

She shook her head. "It is not good that you
be here."

"After one sleep I go."

"And my man?" she demanded, with tremu-
lous eagerness.

Van Brunt shrugged his shoulders. He was
aware of a certain secret shame, of an imper-
sonal sort of shame, and an anger against Fairfax. And he felt the warm blood in his face as
he regarded the young savage. She was just a
woman. That was all—a woman. The whole sor-
did story over again, over and over again, as
old as Eve and young as the last new love-light.

"My man! My man! My man!" she was reiter-
ating vehemently, her face passionately dark,
and the ruthless tenderness of the Eternal
Woman, the Mate-Woman, looking out at him
from her eyes.

"Thom," he said gravely, in English, "you
were born in the Northland forest, and you
have eaten fish and meat, and fought with frost
and famine, and lived simply all the days of
your life. And there are many things, indeed
not simple, which you do not know and cannot
come to understand. You do not know what it
is to long for the fleshpots afar, you cannot understand what it is to yearn for a fair woman's
face. And the woman is fair, Thom, the woman
is nobly fair. You have been woman to this

man, and you have been your all, but your all is very little, very simple. Too little and too simple, and he is an alien man. Him you have never known, you can never know. It is so ordained. You held him in your arms, but you never held his heart, this man with his blurring seasons and his dreams of a barbaric end. Dreams and dream-dust, that is what he has been to you. You clutched at form and gripped shadow, gave yourself to a man and bedded with the wraith of a man. In such manner, of old, did the daughters of men whom the gods found fair. And, Thom, Thom, I should not like to be John Fairfax in the night-watches of the years to come, in the night-watches, when his eyes shall see, not the sun-gloried hair of the woman by his side, but the dark tresses of a mate forsaken in the forests of the North."

Though she did not understand, she had listened with intense attention, as though life hung on his speech. But she caught at her husband's name and cried out in Eskimo:—

"Yes! Yes! Fairfax! My man!"

"Poor little fool, how could he be your man?"

But she could not understand his English tongue, and deemed that she was being trifled with. The dumb, insensate anger of the Mate-Woman flamed in her face, and it almost seemed to the man as though she crouched panther-like for the spring.

He cursed softly to himself and watched the fire fade from her face and the soft luminous glow of the appealing woman spring up, of the appealing woman who foregoes strength and panoplies herself wisely in her weakness.

"He is my man," she said gently. "Never have I known other. It cannot be that I should ever know other. Nor can it be that he should go from me."

"Who has said he shall go from thee?" he demanded sharply, half in exasperation, half in impotence.

"It is for thee to say he shall not go from me," she answered softly, a half-sob in her throat.

Van Brunt kicked the embers of the fire savagely and sat down.

"It is for thee to say. He is my man. Before all women he is my man. Thou art big, thou art strong, and behold, I am very weak. See, I am at thy feet. It is for thee to deal with me. It is for thee."

"Get up!" He jerked her roughly erect and stood up himself. "Thou art a woman. Wherefore the dirt is no place for thee, nor the feet of any man."

"He is my man."

"Then Jesus forgive all men!" Van Brunt cried out passionately.

"He is my man," she repeated monotonously, beseechingly.

"He is my brother," he answered.

"My father is Chief Tantlatch. He is a power over five villages. I will see that the five villages be searched for thy choice of all maidens, that thou mayest stay here by thy brother, and dwell in comfort."

"After one sleep I go."

"And my man?"

"Thy man comes now. Behold!"

From among the gloomy spruces came the light carolling of Fairfax's voice.

As the day is quenched by a sea of fog, so his song smote the light out of her face. "It is the tongue of his own people," she said; "the tongue of his own people."

She turned, with the free movement of a lithe young animal, and made off into the forest.

"It's all fixed," Fairfax called as he came up. "His regal highness will receive you after breakfast."

"Have you told him?" Van Brunt asked.

"No. Nor shall I tell him till we're ready to pull out."

Van Brunt looked with moody affection over the sleeping forms of his men.

"I shall be glad when we are a hundred leagues upon our way," he said.

Thom raised the skin-flap of her father's lodge. Two men sat with him, and the three looked at her with swift interest. But her face betokened nothing as she entered and took seat quietly, without speech. Tantlatch drummed with his knuckles on a spearhaft across his knees, and gazed idly along the path of a sun-ray which pierced a lacing-hole and flung a glittering track across the murky atmosphere of the lodge. To his right, at his shoulder, crouched Chugungatte, the shaman. Both were old men, and the weariness of many years brooded in their eyes. But opposite them sat Keen, a young man and chief favorite in the tribe. He was quick and alert of movement, and his black eyes flashed from face to face in ceaseless scrutiny and challenge.

Silence reigned in the place. Now and again camp noises penetrated, and from the distance, faint and far, like the shadows of voices, came the wrangling of boys in thin shrill tones. A dog thrust his head into the entrance and blinked wolfishly at them for a space, the slaver dripping from his ivory-white fangs. After a time he growled tentatively, and then, awed by the immobility of the human figures, lowered his head and grovelled away backward. Tantlatch glanced apathetically at his daughter.

"And thy man, how is it with him and thee?"

"He sings strange songs," Thom made answer, "and there is a new look on his face."

"So? He hath spoken?"

"Nay, but there is a new look on his face, a new light in his eyes, and with the New-Comer he sits by the fire, and they talk and talk, and the talk is without end."

Chugungatte whispered in his master's ear, and Keen leaned forward from his hips.

"There be something calling him from afar," she went on, "and he seems to sit and listen, and to answer, singing, in his own people's tongue."

Again Chugungatte whispered and Keen leaned forward, and Thom held her speech till her father nodded his head that she might proceed.

"It be known to thee, O Tantlatch, that the wild goose and the swan and the little ringed duck be born here in the low-lying lands. It be known that they go away before the face of the frost to unknown places. And it be known, likewise, that always do they return when the sun is in the land and the waterways are free. Always do they return to where they were born, that new life may go forth. The land calls to them and they come. And now there is another land that calls, and it is calling to my man,—the land where he was born,—and he hath it in mind to answer the call. Yet is he my man. Before all women is he my man."

"Is it well, Tantlatch? Is it well?" Chugungatte demanded, with the hint of menace in his voice.

"Ay, it is well!" Keen cried boldly. "The land calls to its children, and all lands call their children home again. As the wild goose and the swan and the little ringed duck are called, so is called this Stranger Man who has lingered with us and who now must go. Also there be the call of kind. The goose mates with the goose, nor does the swan mate with the little ringed duck. It is not well that the swan should mate with the little ringed duck. Nor is it well that stranger men should mate with the women of our villages. Wherefore I say the man should go, to his own kind, in his own land."

"He is my own man," Thom answered, "and he is a great man."

"Ay, he is a great man." Chugungatte lifted his head with a faint recrudescence of youthful

vigor. "He is a great man, and he put strength
in thy arm, O Tantlatch, and gave thee power,
and made thy name to be feared in the land, to
be feared and to be respected. He is very wise,
and there be much profit in his wisdom. To him
are we beholden for many things,—for the cunning in war and the secrets of the defence of a
village and a rush in the forest, for the discussion in council and the undoing of enemies by
word of mouth and the hard-sworn promise, for
the gathering of game and the making of traps
and the preserving of food, for the curing of
sickness and mending of hurts of trail and fight.
Thou, Tantlatch, wert a lame old man this day,
were it not that the Stranger Man came into our
midst and attended on thee. And ever, when in
doubt on strange questions, have we gone to
him, that out of his wisdom he might make
things clear, and ever has he made things clear.
And there be questions yet to arise, and needs
upon his wisdom yet to come, and we cannot
bear to let him go. It is not well that we should
let him go."

Tantlatch continued to drum on the spearhaft, and gave no sign that he had heard.
Thom studied his face in vain, and Chugungatte seemed to shrink together and droop down
as the weight of years descended upon him
again.

"No man makes my kill." Keen smote his
breast a valorous blow. "I make my own kill. I
am glad to live when I make my own kill.
When I creep through the snow upon the great
moose, I am glad. And when I draw the bow,

so, with my full strength, and drive the arrow fierce and swift and to the heart, I am glad. And the meat of no man's kill tastes as sweet as the meat of my kill. I am glad to live, glad in my own cunning and strength, glad that I am a doer of things, a doer of things for myself. Of what other reason to live than that? Why should I live if I delight not in myself and the things I do? And it is because I delight and am glad that I go forth to hunt and fish, and it is because I go forth to hunt and fish that I grow cunning and strong. The man who stays in the lodge by the fire grows not cunning and strong. He is not made happy in the eating of my kill, nor is living to him a delight. He does not live. And so I say it is well this Stranger Man should go. His wisdom does not make us wise. If he be cunning, there is no need that we be cunning. If need arise, we go to him for his cunning. We eat the meat of his kill, and it tastes unsweet. We merit by his strength, and in it there is no delight. We do not live when he does our living for us. We grow fat and like women, and we are afraid to work, and we forget how to do things for ourselves. Let the man go, O Tantlatch, that we may be men! I am Keen, a man, and I make my own kill!"

Tantlatch turned a gaze upon him in which seemed the vacancy of eternity. Keen waited the decision expectantly; but the lips did not move, and the old chief turned toward his daughter.

"That which be given cannot be taken away," she burst forth. "I was but a girl when this Stranger Man, who is my man, came among us. And I knew not men, or the ways of men, and my heart was in the play of girls, when thou, Tantlatch, thou and none other, didst call me to thee and press me into the arms of the Stranger Man. Thou and none other, Tantlatch; and as thou didst give me to the man, so didst thou give the man to me. He is my man. In my arms has he slept, and from my arms he cannot be taken."

"It were well, O Tantlatch," Keen followed quickly, with a significant glance at Thom, "it were well to remember that that which be given cannot be taken away."

Chugungatte straightened up. "Out of thy youth, Keen, come the words of thy mouth. As for ourselves, O Tantlatch, we be old men and we understand. We, too, have looked into the eyes of women and felt our blood go hot with strange desires. But the years have chilled us, and we have learned the wisdom of the council, the shrewdness of the cool head and hand, and we know that the warm heart be over-warm and prone to rashness. We know that Keen found favor in thy eyes. We know that Thom was promised him in the old days when she was yet a child. And we know that the new days came, and the Stranger Man, and that out of our wisdom and desire for welfare was Thom lost to Keen and the promise broken."

The old shaman paused, and looked directly at the young man.

"And be it known that I, Chugungatte, did advise that the promise be broken."

"Nor have I taken other women to my bed," Keen broke in. "And I have builded my own fire, and cooked my own food, and ground my teeth in my loneliness."

Chugungatte waved his hand that he had not finished. "I am an old man and I speak from understanding. It be good to be strong and grasp for power. It be better to forego power that good come out of it. In the old days I sat at thy shoulder, Tantlatch, and my voice was heard over all in the council, and my advice taken in affairs of moment. And I was strong and held power. Under Tantlatch I was the greatest man. Then came the Stranger Man, and I saw that he was cunning and wise and great. And in that he was wiser and greater than I, it was plain that greater profit should arise from him than from me. And I had thy ear, Tantlatch, and thou didst listen to my words, and the Stranger Man was given power and place and thy daughter, Thom. And the tribe prospered under the new laws in the new days, and so shall it continue to prosper with the Stranger Man in our midst. We be old men, we two, O Tantlatch, thou and I, and this be an affair of head, not heart. Hear my words, Tantlatch! Hear my words! The man remains!"

There was a long silence. The old chief pondered with the massive certitude of God, and Chugungatte seemed to wrap himself in the mists of a great antiquity. Keen looked with yearning upon the woman, and she, unnoting,

held her eyes steadfastly upon her father's face.
The wolf-dog shoved the flap aside again, and
plucking courage at the quiet, wormed forward
on his belly. He sniffed curiously at Thom's
listless hand, cocked ears challengingly at
Chugungatte, and hunched down upon his
haunches before Tantlatch. The spear rattled to
the ground, and the dog, with a frightened
yell, sprang sideways, snapping in mid-air, and
on the second leap cleared the entrance.

Tantlatch looked from face to face, ponder-
ing each one long and carefully. Then he raised
his head, with rude royalty, and gave judgment
in cold and even tones: "The man remains. Let
the hunters be called together. Send a runner
to the next village with word to bring on the
fighting men. I shall not see the New-Comer.
Do thou, Chugungatte, have talk with him. Tell
him he may go at once, if he would go in
peace. And if fight there be, kill, kill, kill, to the
last man; but let my word go forth that no harm
befall our man,—the man whom my daughter
hath wedded. It is well."

Chugungatte rose and tottered out; Thom
followed; but as Keen stooped to the entrance
the voice of Tantlatch stopped him.

"Keen, it were well to hearken to my word.
The man remains. Let no harm befall him."

Because of Fairfax's instructions in the art of
war, the tribesmen did not hurl themselves forward boldly and with clamor. Instead, there
was great restraint and sef-control, and they
were content to advance silently, creeping and

crawling from shelter to shelter. By the river bank, and partly protected by a narrow open space, crouched the Crees and *voyageurs*. Their eyes could see nothing, and only in vague ways did their ears hear, but they felt the thrill of life which ran through the forest, the indistinct, indefinable movement of an advancing host.

"Damn them," Fairfax muttered. "They've never faced powder, but I taught them the trick."

Avery Van Brunt laughed, knocked the ashes out of his pipe, and put it carefully away with the pouch, and loosened the hunting-knife in its sheath at his hip.

"Wait," he said. "We'll wither the face of the charge and break their hearts."

"They'll rush scattered if they remember my teaching.'

"Let them. Magazine rifles were made to pump. We'll—good! First blood! Extra tobacco, Loon!"

Loon, a Cree, had spotted an exposed shoulder and with a stinging bullet apprised its owner of his discovery.

"If we can tease them into breaking forward," Fairfax muttered,—"if we can only tease them into breaking forward."

Van Brunt saw a head peer from behind a distant tree, and with a quick shot sent the man sprawling to the ground in a death struggle. Michael potted a third, and Fairfax and the rest took a hand, firing at every exposure and into each clump of agitated brush. In crossing one little swale out of cover, five of the tribesmen remained on their faces, and to the left, where the covering was sparse, a dozen men were struck. But they took the punishment with sullen steadiness, coming on cautiously, deliberately, without haste and without lagging.

Ten minutes later, when they were quite close, all movement was suspended, the advance ceased abruptly, and the quietness that followed was portentous, threatening. Only could be seen the green and gold of the woods and undergrowth, shivering and trembling to the first faint puffs of the day-wind. The wan white morning sun mottled the earth with long shadows and streaks of light. A wounded man lifted his head and crawled painfully out of the swale, Michael following him with his rifle but forebearing to shoot. A whistle ran along the invisible line from left to right, and a flight of arrows arched through the air.

"Get ready," Van Brunt commanded, a new metallic note in his voice. "Now!"

They broke cover simultaneously. The forest heaved into sudden life. A great yell went up, and the rifles barked back sharp defiance. Tribesmen knew their deaths in mid-leap, and as they fell, their brothers surged over them in a roaring, irresistible wave. In the forefront of the rush, hair flying and arms swinging free, flashing past the tree-trunks, and leaping the obstructing logs, came Thom. Fairfax sighted on her and almost pulled trigger ere he knew her.

"The woman! Don't shoot!" he cried. "See! She is unarmed!"

The Crees never heard, nor Michael and his brother *voyageur*, nor Van Brunt, who was keeping one shell continuously in the air. But Thom bore straight on, unharmed, at the heels of a skin-clad hunter who had veered in before her from the side. Fairfax emptied his magazine into the men to right and left of her, and swung his rifle to meet the big hunter. But the man, seeming to recognize him, swerved suddenly aside and plunged his spear into the body of Michael. On the moment Thom had one arm passed around her husband's neck, and twisting half about, with voice and gesture was splitting the mass of charging warriors. A score of men hurled past on either side, and Fairfax, for a brief instant's space, stood looking upon her and her bronze beauty, thrilling, exulting, stirred to unknown deeps, visioning strange things, dreaming, immortally dreaming. Snatches and scraps of old-world philosophies and new-world ethics floated through his mind, and things wonderfully concrete and wofully incongruous—hunting scenes, stretches of sombre forest, vastnesses of silent snow, the glittering of ballroom lights, great galleries and lecture halls, a fleeting shimmer of glistening test-tubes, long rows of book-lined shelves, the throb of machinery and the roar of traffic, a fragment of forgotten song, faces of dear women and old chums, a lonely watercourse amid upstanding peaks, a shattered boat on a pebbly strand, quiet moonlit fields, fat vales, the smell of hay. . . .

A hunter, struck between the eyes with a rifle-ball, pitched forward lifeless, and with the momentum of his charge slid along the ground. Fairfax came back to himself. His comrades, those that lived, had been swept far back among the trees beyond. He could hear the fierce "Hia! Hia!" of the hunters as they closed in and cut and thrust with their weapons of bone and ivory. The cries of the stricken men smote him like blows. He knew the fight was over, the cause was lost, but all his race traditions and race loyalty impelled him into the welter that he might die at least with his kind.

"My man! My man!" Thom cried. "Thou art safe!"

He tried to struggle on, but her dead weight clogged his steps.

"There is no need! They are dead, and life be good!"

She held him close around the neck and twined her limbs about his till he tripped and stumbled, reeled violently to recover footing, tripped again, and fell backward to the ground. His head struck a jutting root, and he was half-stunned and could struggle but feebly. In the fall she had heard the feathered swish of an arrow darting past, and she covered his body with hers, as with a shield, her arms holding him tightly, her face and lips pressed upon his neck.

Then it was that Keen rose up from a tangled thicket a score of feet away. He looked about him with care. The fight had swept on and the cry of the last man was dying away. There was no one to see. He fitted an arrow to the string and glanced at the man and woman. Between her breast and arm the flesh of the man's side showed white. Keen bent the bow and drew back the arrow to its head. Twice he did so, calmly and for certainty, and then drove the bone-barbed missile straight home to the white flesh, gleaming yet more white in the dark-armed, dark-breasted embrace.

THE GOD OF
HIS FATHERS

On every hand stretched the forest primeval,—the home of noisy comedy and silent tragedy. Here the struggle for survival continued to wage with all its ancient brutality. Briton and Russian were still to overlap in the Land of the Rainbow's End—and this was the very heart of it—nor had Yankee gold yet purchased its vast domain. The wolf-pack still clung to the flank of the cariboo-herd, singling out the weak and the big with calf, and pulling them down as remorselessly as were it a thousand, thousand generations into the past. The sparse aborigines still acknowledged the rule of their chiefs and medicine men, drove out bad spirits, burned their witches, fought their neighbors, and ate their enemies with a relish which spoke well of their bellies. But it was at the moment when the stone age was drawing to a close. Already, over unknown trails and chartless wildernesses, were the harbingers of the steel arriving,—fair-faced, blue-eyed, indomitable men, incarnations of the unrest of their

race. By accident or design, single-handed and
in twos and threes, they came from no one
knew whither, and fought, or died, or passed
on, no one knew whence. The priests raged
against them, the chiefs called forth their fighting men, and stone clashed with steel; but to
little purpose. Like water seeping from some
mighty reservoir, they trickled through the
dark forests and mountain passes, threading
the highways in bark canoes, or with their moccasined feet breaking trail for the wolf-dogs.
They came of a great breed, and their mothers
were many; but the fur-clad denizens of the
Northland had this yet to learn. So many an
unsung wanderer fought his last and died under the cold fire of the aurora, as did his brothers in burning sands and reeking jungles, and
as they shall continue to do till in the fulness of
time the destiny of their race be achieved. It
was near twelve. Along the northern horizon a
rosy glow, fading to the west and deepening to
the east, marked the unseen dip of the midnight sun. The gloaming and the dawn were so
commingled that there was no night,—simply a
wedding of day with day, a scarcely percepti-
ble blending of two circles of the sun. A kildee
timidly chirped good-night; the full, rich throat
of a robin proclaimed good-morrow. From an
island on the breast of the Yukon a colony of
wild fowl voiced its interminable wrongs, while
a loon laughed mockingly back across a still
stretch of river.

In the foreground, against the bank of a lazy
eddy, birch-bark canoes were lined two and

three deep. Ivory-bladed spears, bone-barbed arrows, buckskin-thonged bows, and simple basket-woven traps bespoke the fact that in the muddy current of the river the salmon-run was on. In the background, from the tangle of skin tents and drying frames, rose the voices of the fisher folk. Bucks skylarked with bucks or flirted with the maidens, while the older squaws, shut out from this by virtue of having fulfilled the end of their existence in reproduction, gossiped as they braided rope from the green roots of trailing vines. At their feet their naked progeny played and squabbled, or rolled in the muck with the tawny wolf-dogs.

To one side of the encampment, and conspicuously apart from it, stood a second camp of two tents. But it was a white man's camp. If nothing else, the choice of position at least bore convincing evidence of this. In case of offence, it commanded the Indian quarters a hundred yards away; of defence, a rise to the ground and the cleared intervening space; and last, of defeat, the swift slope of a score of yards to the canoes below. From one of the tents came the petulant cry of a sick child and the crooning song of a mother. In the open, over the smouldering embers of a fire, two men held talk.

"Eh? I love the church like a good son. *Bien!* So great a love that my days have been spent in fleeing away from her, and my nights in dreaming dreams of reckoning. Look you!" The half-breed's voice rose to an angry snarl. "I am Red River born. My father was white—as white as you. But you are Yankee, and he was British

bred, and a gentleman's son. And my mother
was the daughter of a chief, and I was a man.
Ay, and one had to look the second time to see
what manner of blood ran in my veins; for I
lived with the whites, and was one of them, and
my father's heart beat in me. It happened there
was a maiden—white—who looked on me with
kind eyes. Her father had much land and many
horses; also he was a big man among his people,
and his blood was the blood of the French. He
said the girl knew not her own mind, and talked
overmuch with her, and became wroth that such
things should be.

"But she knew her mind, for we came quick
before the priest. And quicker had come her father, with lying words, false promises, I know
not what; so that the priest stiffened his neck
and would not make us that we might live one
with the other. As at the beginning it was the
church which would not bless my birth, so now
it was the church which refused me marriage
and put the blood of men upon my hands.
Bien! Thus have I cause to love the church. So
I struck the priest on his woman's mouth, and
we took swift horses, the girl and I, to Fort
Pierre, where was a minister of good heart. But
hot on our trail was her father, and brothers,
and other men he had gathered to him. And we
fought, our horses on the run, till I emptied
three saddles and the rest drew off and went on
to Fort Pierre. Then we took east, the girl and
I, to the hills and forests, and we lived one with
the other, and we were not married,—the work
of the good church which I love like a son.

"But mark you, for this is the strangeness of woman, the way of which no man may understand. One of the saddles I emptied was that of her father's, and the hoofs of those who came behind had pounded him into the earth. This we saw, the girl and I, and this I had forgot had she not remembered. And in the quiet of the evening, after the day's hunt were done, it came between us, and in the silence of the night when we lay beneath the stars and should have been one. It was there always. She never spoke, but it sat by our fire and held us ever apart. She tried to put it aside, but at such times it would rise up till I could read it in the look of her eyes, in the very in-take of her breath.

"So in the end she bore me a child, a woman-child, and died. Then I went among my mother's people, that it might nurse at a warm breast and live. But my hands were wet with the blood of men, look you, because of the church, wet with the blood of men. And the Riders of the North came for me, but my mother's brother, who was then chief in his own right, hid me and gave me horses and food. And we went away, my woman-child and I, even to the Hudson Bay Country, where white men were few and the questions they asked not many. And I worked for the company as a hunter, as a guide, as a driver of dogs, till my woman-child was become a woman, tall, and slender, and fair to the eye.

"You know the winter, long and lonely, breeding evil thoughts and bad deeds. The Chief Factor was a hard man, and bold. And he was not such that a woman would delight in looking upon. But he cast eyes upon my woman-child who was become a woman. Mother of God! he sent me away on a long trip with the dogs, that he might—you understand, he was a hard man and without heart. She was most white, and her soul was white, and a good woman, and—well, she died.

"It was bitter cold the night of my return, and I had been away months, and the dogs were limping sore when I came to the fort. The Indians and breeds looked on in silence, and I felt the fear of I knew not what, but I said nothing till the dogs were fed and I had eaten as a man with work before him should. Then I spoke up, demanding the word, and they shrank from me, afraid of my anger and what I should do; but the story came out, the pitiful story, word for word and act for act, and they marvelled that I should be so quiet.

"When they had done I went to the Factor's house, calmer than now in the telling of it. He had been afraid and called upon the breeds to help him; but they were not pleased with the deed, and had left him to lie on the bed he had made. So he had fled to the house of the priest. Thither I followed. But when I was come to that place, the priest stood in my way, and spoke soft words, and said a man in anger should go neither to the right nor left, but straight to God. I asked by the right of a father's wrath that he give me past, but he said only over his body, and besought with me to pray. Look you, it was the church, always the church; for I passed over his body and sent the Factor to meet my woman-child before his god, which is a bad god, and the god of the white men.

"Then was there hue and cry, for word was sent to the station below, and I came away. Through the land of the Great Slave, down the Valley of the Mackenzie to the never-opening ice, over the White Rockies, past the Great Curve of the Yukon, even to this place did I come. And from that day to this, yours is the first face of my father's people I have looked upon. May it be the last! These people, which are my people, are a simple folk, and I have been raised to honor among them. My word is their law, and their priests but do my bidding, else would I not suffer them. When I speak for them I speak for myself. We ask to be let alone. We do not want your kind. If we permit you to sit by our fires, after you will come your church, your priests, and your gods. And know this, for each white man who comes to my village, him will I make deny his god. You are the first, and I give you grace. So it were well you go, and go quickly."

"I am not responsible for my brothers," the second man spoke up, filling his pipe in a meditative manner. Hay Stockard was at times as thoughtful of speech as he was wanton of action; but only at times.

"But I know your breed," responded the other. "Your brothers are many, and it is you and yours who break the trail for them to follow. In time they shall come to possess the land, but not in my time. Already, have I heard, are they on the head-reaches of the Great River, and far away below are the Russians."

Hay Stockard lifted his head with a quick start. This was startling geographical information. The Hudson Bay post at Fort Yukon had other notions concerning the course of the river, believing it to flow into the Arctic.

"Then the Yukon empties into Bering Sea?" he asked.

"I do not know, but below there are Russians, many Russians. Which is neither here nor there. You may go on and see for yourself; you may go back to your brothers; but up the Koyukuk you shall not go while the priests and fighting men do my bidding. Thus do I command, I, Baptiste the Red, whose word is law and who am head man over this people."

"And should I not go down to the Russians, or back to my brothers?"

"Then shall you go swift-footed before your god, which is a bad god, and the god of the white men."

The red sun shot up above the northern skyline, dripping and bloody. Baptiste the Red came to his feet, nodded curtly, and went back to his camp amid the crimson shadows and the singing of the robins.

Hay Stockard finished his pipe by the fire, picturing in smoke and coal the unknown upper reaches of the Koyukuk, the strange stream which ended here its arctic travels and merged its waters with the muddy Yukon flood. Somewhere up there, if the dying words of a ship-wrecked sailorman who had made the fearful overland journey were to be believed, and if the vial of golden grains in his pouch attested anything,—somewhere up there, in that home of winter, stood the Treasure House of the North. And as keeper of the gate, Baptiste the Red, English half-breed and renegade, barred the way.

"Bah!" He kicked the embers apart and rose to his full height, arms lazily outstretched, facing the flushing north with careless soul.

* * *

Hay Stockard swore, harshly, in the rugged monosyllables of his mother tongue. His wife lifted her gaze from the pots and pans, and followed his in a keen scrutiny of the river. She was a woman of the Teslin Country, wise in the ways of her husband's vernacular when it grew intensive. From the slipping of a snowshoe thong to the forefront of sudden death, she could gauge occasion by the pitch and volume of his blasphemy. So she knew the present occasion merited attention. A long canoe, with paddles flashing back the rays of the westering sun, was crossing the current from above and urging in for the eddy. Hay Stockard watched it intently. Three men rose and dipped, rose and dipped, in rhythmical precision; but a red bandanna, wrapped about the head of one, caught and held his eye.

"Bill!" he called. "Oh, Bill!"

A shambling, loose-jointed giant rolled out of one of the tents, yawning and rubbing the sleep from his eyes. Then he sighted the strange canoe and was wide awake on the instant.

"By the jumping Methuselah! That damned sky-pilot!"

Hay Stockard nodded his head bitterly, half-reached for his rifle, then shrugged his shoulders.

"Pot-shot him," Bill suggested, "and settle the thing out of hand. He'll spoil us sure if we don't." But the other declined this drastic measure and turned away, at the same time bidding the woman return to her work, and calling Bill back from the bank. The two Indians in the canoe moored it on the edge of the eddy, while its white occupant, conspicuous by his gorgeous head-gear, came up the bank.

"Like Paul of Tarsus, I give you greeting. Peace be unto you and grace before the Lord."

His advances were met sullenly, and without speech.

"To you, Hay Stockard, blasphemer and Philistine, greeting. In your heart is the lust of Mammon, in your mind cunning devils, in your tent this woman whom you live with in adultery; yet of these divers sins, even here in the wilderness, I, Sturges Owen, apostle to the Lord, bid you to repent and cast from you your iniquities."

"Save your cant! Save your cant!" Hay Stockard broke in testily. "You'll need all you've got, and more, for Red Baptiste over yonder."

He waved his hand toward the Indian camp, where the half-breed was looking steadily across, striving to make out the new-comers. Sturges Owen, disseminator of light and apostle to the Lord, stepped to the edge of the steep and commanded his men to bring up the camp outfit. Stockard followed him.

"Look here," he demanded, plucking the missionary by the shoulder and twirling him about. "Do you value your hide?"

"My life is in the Lord's keeping, and I do but work in His vineyard," he replied solemnly.

"Oh, stow that! Are you looking for a job of martyrship?"

"If He so wills."

"Well, you'll find it right here, but I'm going to give you some advice first. Take it or leave it. If you stop here, you'll be cut off in the midst of your labors. And not you alone, but your men, Bill, my wife—"

"Who is a daughter of Belial and hearkeneth not to the true Gospel."

"And myself. Not only do you bring trouble upon yourself, but upon us. I was frozen in with you last winter, as you will well recollect, and I know you for a good man and a fool. If you think it your duty to strive with the heathen, well and good; but do exercise some wit in the way you go about it. This man, Red Baptiste, is no Indian. He comes of our common stock, is as bull-necked as I ever dared be, and as wild a fanatic the one way as you are the other. When you two come together, hell'll be to pay, and I don't care to be mixed up in it.

Understand? So take my advice and go away. If you go down-stream, you'll fall in with the Russians. There's bound to be Greek priests among them, and they'll see you safe through to Bering Sea,—that's where the Yukon empties,—and from there it won't be hard to get back to civilization. Take my word for it and get out of here as fast as God'll let you."

"He who carries the Lord in his heart and the Gospel in his hand hath no fear of the machinations of man or devil," the missionary answered stoutly. "I will see this man and wrestle with him. One backslider returned to the fold is a greater victory than a thousand heathen. He who is strong for evil can be as mighty for good, witness Saul when he journeyed up to Damascus to bring Christian captives to Jerusalem. And the voice of the Saviour came to him, crying, 'Saul, Saul, why persecutest thou me?' And therewith Paul arrayed himself on the side of the Lord, and thereafter was most mighty in the saving of souls. And even as thou, Paul of Tarsus, even so do I work in the vineyard of the Lord, bearing trials and tribulations, scoffs and sneers, stripes and punishments, for His dear sake."

"Bring up the little bag with the tea and a kettle of water," he called the next instant to his boatmen; "not forgetting the haunch of cariboo and the mixing-pan."

When his men, converts by his own hand, had gained the bank, the trio fell to their knees, hands and backs burdened with camp equipage, and offered up thanks for their passage through the wilderness and their safe arrival. Hay Stockard looked upon the function with sneering disapproval, the romance and solemnity of it lost to his matter-of-fact soul. Baptiste the Red, still gazing across, recognized the familiar postures, and remembered the girl who had shared his star-roofed couch in the hills and forests, and the woman-child who lay somewhere by bleak Hudson's Bay.

*   *   *

"Confound it, Baptiste, couldn't think of it. Not for a moment. Grant that this man is a fool and of small use in the nature of things, but still, you know, I can't give him up."

Hay Stockard paused, striving to put into speech the rude ethics of his heart.

"He's worried me, Baptiste, in the past and now, and caused me all manner of troubles; but can't you see, he's my own breed—white—and—and—why, I couldn't buy my life with his, not if he was a nigger."

"So be it," Baptiste the Red made answer. "I have given you grace and choice. I shall come presently, with my priests and fighting men, and either shall I kill you, or you deny your god. Give up the priest to my pleasure, and you shall depart in peace. Otherwise your trail ends here. My people are against you to the babies. Even now have the children stolen away your canoes."

He pointed down to the river. Naked boys had slipped down the water from the point above, cast loose the canoes, and by then had worked them into the current. When they had drifted out of rifle-shot they clambered over the sides and paddled ashore.

"Give me the priest, and you may have them back again. Come! Speak your mind, but without haste."

Stockard shook his head. His glance dropped to the woman of the Teslin Country with his boy at her breast, and he would have wavered had he not lifted his eyes to the man before him.

"I am not afraid," Sturges Owen spoke up. "The Lord bears me in his right hand, and alone am I ready to go into the camp of the unbeliever. It is not too late. Faith may move mountains. Even in the eleventh hour may I win his soul to the true righteousness."

"Trip the beggar up and make him fast," Bill whispered hoarsely in the ear of his leader, while the missionary kept the floor and wrestled with the heathen. "Make him hostage, and bore him if they get ugly."

"No," Stockard answered. "I gave him my word that he could speak with us unmolested. Rules of warfare, Bill; rules of warfare. He's been on the square, given us warning, and all that, and—why, damn it, man, I can't break my word!"

"He'll keep his, never fear."

"Don't doubt it, but I won't let a half-breed outdo me in fair dealing. Why not do what he wants,—give him the missionary and be done with it?"

"No-no," Bill hesitated doubtfully.

"Shoe pinches, eh?"

Bill flushed a little and dropped the discussion. Baptiste the Red was still waiting the final decision. Stockard went up to him.

"It's this way, Baptiste. I came to your village minded to go up the Koyukuk. I intended no wrong. My heart was clean of evil. It is still clean. Along comes this priest, as you call him. I didn't bring him here. He'd have come whether I was here or not. But now that he is here, being of my people, I've got to stand by him. And I'm going to. Further, it will be no child's play. When you have done, your village will be silent and empty, your people wasted as after a famine. True, we will be gone; likewise the pick of your fighting men—"

"But those who remain shall be in peace, nor shall the word of strange gods and the tongues of strange priests be buzzing in their ears."

Both men shrugged their shoulders and turned away, the half-breed going back to his own camp. The missionary called his two men to him, and they fell into prayer. Stockard and Bill attacked the few standing pines with their axes, felling them into convenient breastworks. The child had fallen asleep, so the woman placed it on a heap of furs and lent a hand in fortifying the camp. Three sides were thus defended, the steep declivity at the rear precluding attack from that direction. When these arrangements had been completed, the two men stalked into the open, clearing away, here and there, the scattered underbrush. From the

opposing camp came the booming of war-
drums and the voices of the priests stirring the
people to anger.

"Worst of it is they'll come in rushes," Bill
complained as they walked back with shouldered axes.

"And wait till midnight, when the light gets
dim for shooting."

"Can't start the ball a-rolling too early, then."
Bill exchanged the axe for a rifle, and took a
careful rest. One of the medicine-men, towering
above his tribesmen, stood out distinctly. Bill
drew a bead on him.

"All ready?" he asked.

Stockard opened the ammunition box, placed
the woman where she could reload in safety,
and gave the word. The medicine-man dropped.
For a moment there was silence, then a wild
howl went up and a flight of bone arrows fell
short.

"I'd like to take a look at the beggar," Bill remarked, throwing a fresh shell into place. "I'll
swear I drilled him clean between the eyes."

"Didn't work." Stockard shook his head
gloomily. Baptiste had evidently quelled the
more warlike of his followers, and instead of pre-
cipitating an attack in the bright light of day,
the shot had caused a hasty exodus, the Indians
drawing out of the village beyond the zone of
fire.

In the full tide of his proselyting fervor,
borne along by the hand of God, Sturges Owen
would have ventured alone into the camp of
the unbeliever, equally prepared for miracle or

martyrdom; but in the waiting which ensued, the fever of conviction died away gradually, as the natural man asserted itself. Physical fear replaced spiritual hope; the love of life, the love of God. It was no new experience. He could feel his weakness coming on, and knew it of old time. He had struggled against it and been overcome by it before. He remembered when the other men had driven their paddles like mad in the van of a roaring iceflood, how, at the critical moment in a panic of worldly terror, he had dropped his paddle and besought wildly with his God for pity. And there were other times. The recollection was not pleasant. It brought shame to him that his spirit should be so weak and his flesh so strong. But the love of life! the love of life! He could not strip it from him. Because of it had his dim ancestors perpetuated their line; because of it was he destined to perpetuate his. His courage, if courage it might be called, was bred of fanaticism. The courage of Stockard and Bill was the adherence to deep-rooted ideals. Not that the love of life was less, but the love of race tradition more; not that they were unafraid to die, but that they were brave enough not to live at the price of shame.

The missionary rose, for the moment swayed by the mood of sacrifice. He half crawled over the barricade to proceed to the other camp, but sank back, a trembling mass, wailing: "As the spirit moves! As the spirit moves! Whe am I that I should set aside the judgments of God? Before the foundations of the world were all things written in the book of life. Worm that I am, shall I erase the page or any portion thereof? As God wills, so shall the spirit move!"

Bill reached over, plucked him to his feet, and shook him, fiercely, silently. Then he dropped the bundle of quivering nerves and turned his attention to the two converts. But they showed little fright and a cheerful alacrity in preparing for the coming passage at arms.

Stockard, who had been talking in undertones with the Teslin woman, now turned to the missionary.

"Fetch him over here," he commanded of Bill.

"Now," he ordered, when Sturges Owen had been duly deposited before him, "make us man and wife, and be lively about it." Then he added apologetically to Bill: "No telling how it's to end, so I just thought I'd get my affairs straightened up."

The woman obeyed the behest of her white lord. To her the ceremony was meaningless. By her lights she was his wife, and had been from the day they first foregathered. The converts served as witnesses. Bill stood over the missionary, prompting him when he stumbled. Stockard put the responses in the woman's mouth, and when the time came, for want of better, ringed her finger with thumb and forefinger of his own.

"Kiss the bride!" Bill thundered, and Sturges Owen was too weak to disobey.

"Now baptize the child!"

"Neat and tidy," Bill commented.

"Gathering the proper outfit for a new trail," the father explained, taking the boy from the mother's arms. "I was grub-staked, once, into the Cascades, and had everything in the kit except salt. Never shall forget it. And if the woman and the kid cross the divide to-night they might as well be prepared for pot-luck. A long shot, Bill, between ourselves, but nothing lost if it misses."

A cup of water served the purpose, and the child was laid away in a secure corner of the barricade. The men built the fire, and the evening meal was cooked.

The sun hurried round to the north, sinking closer to the horizon. The heavens in that quarter grew red and bloody. The shadows lengthened, the light dimmed, and in the sombre recesses of the forest life slowly died away. Even the wild fowl in the river softened their raucous chatter and feigned the nightly farce of going to bed. Only the tribesmen increased their clamor, war-drums booming and voices raised in savage folk songs. But as the sun dipped they ceased their tumult. The rounded hush of midnight was complete. Stockard rose to his knees and peered over the logs. Once the child wailed in pain and disconcerted him. The mother bent over it, but it slept again. The silence was interminable, profound. Then, of a sudden, the robins burst into full-throated song. The night had passed.

A flood of dark figures boiled across the open. Arrows whistled and bow-thongs sang. The shrill-tongued rifles answered back. A spear,

and a mighty cast, transfixed the Teslin woman
as she hovered above the child. A spent arrow,
diving between the logs, lodged in the missionary's arm.

There was no stopping the rush. The middle
distance was cumbered with bodies, but the
rest surged on, breaking against and over the
barricade like an ocean wave. Sturges Owen
fled to the tent, while the men were swept from
their feet, buried beneath the human tide. Hay
Stockard alone regained the surface, flinging
the tribesmen aside like yelping curs. He had
managed to seize an axe. A dark hand grasped
the child by a naked foot, and drew it from
beneath its mother. At arm's length its puny
body circled through the air, dashing to death
against the logs. Stockard clove the man to the
chin and fell to clearing space. The ring of savage faces closed in, raining upon him spear-
thrusts and bone-barbed arrows. The sun shot
up, and they swayed back and forth in the
crimson shadows. Twice, with his axe blocked
by too deep a blow, they rushed him; but each
time he flung them clear. They fell underfoot
and he trampled dead and dying, the way slippery with blood. And still the day brightened
and the robins sang. Then they drew back from
him in awe, and he leaned breathless upon his
axe.

"Blood of my soul!" cried Baptiste the Red.
"But thou art a man. Deny thy god, and thou
shalt yet live."

Stockard swore his refusal, feebly but with
grace.

"Behold! A woman!" Sturges Owen had been brought before the half-breed.

Beyond a scratch on the arm, he was uninjured, but his eyes roved about him in an ecstasy of fear. The heroic figure of the blasphemer, bristling with wounds and arrows, leaning defiantly upon his axe, indifferent, indomitable, superb, caught his wavering vision. And he felt a great envy of the man who could go down serenely to the dark gates of death. Surely Christ, and not he, Sturges Owen, had been moulded in such manner. And why not he? He felt dimly the curse of ancestry, the feebleness of spirit which had come down to him out of the past, and he felt an anger at the creative force, symbolize it as he would, which had formed him, its servant, so weakly. For even a stronger man, this anger and the stress of circumstance were sufficient to breed apostasy, and for Sturges Owen it was inevitable. In the fear of man's anger he would dare the wrath of God. He had been raised up to serve the Lord only that he might be cast down. He had been given faith without the strength of faith; he had been given spirit without the power of spirit. It was unjust.

"Where now is thy god?" the half-breed demanded.

"I do not know." He stood straight and rigid, like a child repeating a catechism.

"Hast thou then a god at all?"

"I had."

"And now?"

"No."

Hay Stockard swept the blood from his eyes and laughed. The missionary looked at him curiously, as in a dream. A feeling of infinite distance came over him, as though of a great remove. In that which had transpired, and which was to transpire, he had no part. He was a spectator—at a distance, yes, at a distance. The words of Baptiste came to him faintly:—

"Very good. See that this man go free, and that no harm befall him. Let him depart in peace Give him a canoe and food. Set his face toward the Russians, that he may tell their priests of Baptiste the Red, in whose country there is no god."

They led him to the edge of the steep, where they paused to witness the final tragedy. The half-breed turned to Hay Stockard.

"There is no god," he prompted.

The man laughed in reply. One of the young men poised a war-spear for the cast.

"Hast thou a god?"

"Ay, the God of my fathers."

He shifted the axe for a better grip. Baptiste the Red gave the sign, and the spear hurtled full against his breast. Sturges Owen saw the ivory head stand out beyond his back, saw the man sway, laughing, and snap the shaft short as he fell upon it. Then he went down to the river, that he might carry to the Russians the message of Baptiste the Red, in whose country there was no god.

from "THE SEA WOLF"

The chagrin Wolf Larsen felt from being ignored by Maud Brewster and me in the conversation at table had to express itself in some fashion, and it fell to Thomas Mugridge to be the victim. He had not mended his ways nor his shirt, though the latter he contended he had changed. The garment itself did not bear out the assertion, nor did the accumulations of grease on stove and pot and pan attest a general cleanliness.

"I've given you warning, Cooky," Wolf Larsen said, "and now you've got to take your medicine."

Mugridge's face turned white under its sooty veneer, and when Wolf Larsen called for a rope and a couple of men, the miserable Cockney fled wildly out of the galley and dodged and ducked about the deck with the grinning crew in pursuit. Few things could have been more to their liking than to give him a tow over the side, for to the forecastle he had sent messes and concoctions of the vilest order. Conditions favored the undertaking. The *Ghost* was slipping through the water at no more than three

miles an hour, and the sea was fairly calm. But
Mugridge had little stomach for a dip in it.
Possibly he had seen men towed before.
Besides, the water was frightfully cold, and his
was anything but a rugged constitution.

As usual, the watches below and the hunters
turned out for what promised sport. Mugridge
seemed to be in rabid fear of the water, and he
exhibited a nimbleness and speed we did not
dream he possessed. Cornered in the right-
angle of the poop and galley, he sprang like a
cat to the top of the cabin and ran aft. But his
pursuers forestalling him, he doubled back
across the cabin, passed over the galley, and
gained the deck by means of the steerage-
scuttle. Straight forward he raced, the boat-pul-
ler Harrison at his heels and gaining on him.
But Mugridge, leaping suddenly, caught the
jib-boom-lift. It happened in an instant. Holding his weight by his arms, and in mid-air doubling his body at the hips, he let fly with both
feet. The oncoming Harrison caught the kick
squarely in the pit of the stomach, groaned in-
voluntarily, and doubled up and sank backward to the deck.

Hand-clapping and roars of laughter from
the hunters greeted the exploit, while
Mugridge, eluding half of his pursuers at the
foremast, ran aft and through the remainder
like a runner on the football field. Straight aft
he held, to the poop and along the poop to the
stern. So great was his speed that as he curved
past the corner of the cabin he slipped and fell.
Nilson was standing at the wheel, and the

Cockney's hurtling body struck his legs. Both went down together, but Mugridge alone arose. By some freak of pressures, his frail body had snapped the strong man's leg like a pipestem.

Parsons took the wheel, and the pursuit continued. Round and round the decks they went, Mugridge sick with fear, the sailors hallooing and shouting directions to one another, and the hunters bellowing encouragement and laughter. Mugridge went down on the fore-hatch under three men; but he emerged from the mass like an eel, bleeding at the mouth, the offending shirt ripped into tatters, and sprang for the main-rigging. Up he went, clear up, beyond the ratlines, to the very masthead.

Half a dozen sailors swarmed to the crosstrees after him, where they clustered and waited while two of their number, Oofty-Oofty and Black, (who was Latimer's boatsteerer), continued up the thin steel stays, lifting their bodies higher and higher by means of their arms.

It was a perilous undertaking, for, at a height of over a hundred feet from the deck, holding on by their hands, they were not in the best of positions to protect themselves from Mugridge's feet. And Mugridge kicked savagely, till the Kanaka, hanging on with one hand, seized the Cockney's foot with the other. Black duplicated the performance a moment later with the other foot. Then the three writhed together in a swaying tangle, struggling, sliding, and falling into the arms of their mates on the crosstrees.

The aerial battle was over, and Thomas

Mugridge, whining and gibbering, his mouth
flecked with bloody foam, was brought down to
deck. Wolf Larsen rove a bowline in a piece of
rope and slipped it under his shoulders. Then
he was carried aft and flung into the sea.
Forty,—fifty,—sixty feet of line ran out, when
Wolf Larsen cried "Belay!" Oofty-Oofty took a
turn on a bitt, the rope tautened, and the *Ghost*,
lunging onward, jerked the cook to the surface.

It was a pitiful spectacle. Though he could
not drown, and was nine-lived in addition, he
was suffering all the agonies of half-drowning.
The *Ghost* was going very slowly, and when
her stern lifted on a wave and she slipped forward she pulled the wretch to the surface and
gave him a moment in which to breathe; but
between each lift the stern fell, and while the
bow lazily climbed the next wave the line
slacked and he sank beneath.

I had forgotten the existence of Maud
Brewster, and I remembered her with a start as
she stepped lightly beside me. It was her first
time on deck since she had come aboard. A
dead silence greeted her appearance.

"What is the cause of the merriment?" she
asked.

"Ask Captain Larsen," I answered com-
posedly and coldly, though inwardly my blood
was boiling at the thought that she should be
witness to such brutality.

She took my advice and was turning to put it
into execution, when her eyes lighted on
Oofty-Oofty, immediately before her, his body

instinct with alertness and grace as he held the turn of the rope.

"Are you fishing?" she asked him.

He made no reply. His eyes, fixed intently on the sea astern, suddenly flashed.

"Shark ho, sir!" he cried.

"Heave in! Lively! All hands tail on!" Wolf Larsen shouted, springing himself to the rope in advance of the quickest.

Mugridge had heard the Kanaka's warning cry and was screaming madly. I could see a black fin cutting the water and making for him with greater swiftness than he was being pulled aboard. It was an even toss whether the shark or we would get him, and it was a matter of moments. When Mugridge was directly beneath us, the stern descended the slope of a passing wave, thus giving the advantage to the shark. The fin disappeared. The belly flashed white in a swift upward rush. Almost equally swift, but not quite, was Wolf Larsen. He threw his strength into one tremendous jerk. The Cockney's body left the water; so did part of the shark's. He drew up his legs, and the man-eater seemed no more than barely to touch one foot, sinking back into the water with a splash. But at the moment of contact Thomas Mugridge cried out. Then he came in like a fresh-caught fish on a line, clearing the rail generously and striking the deck in a heap, on hands and knees, and rolling over.

But a fountain of blood was gushing forth. The right foot was missing, amputated neatly at the ankle. I looked instantly to Maud

Brewster. Her face was white, her eyes dilated with horror. She was gazing, not at Thomas Mugridge, but at Wolf Larsen. And he was aware of it, for he said, with one of his short laughs:

"Man-play, Miss Brewster. Somewhat rougher, I warrant, than what you have been used to, but still—man-play. The shark was not in the reckoning. It—"

But at this juncture, Mugridge, who had lifted his head and ascertained the extent of his loss, floundered over on the deck and buried his teeth in Wolf Larsen's leg. Wolf Larsen stooped, coolly, to the Cockney, and pressed with thumb and finger at the rear of the jaws and below the ears. The jaws opened with reluctance, and Wolf Larsen stepped free.

"As I was saying," he went on, as though nothing unwonted had happened, "the shark was not in the reckoning. It was—ahem—shall we say Providence?"

She gave no sign that she had heard, though the expression of her eyes changed to one of inexpressible loathing as she started to turn away. She no more than started, for she swayed and tottered, and reached her hand weakly out to mine. I caught her in time to save her from falling, and helped her to a seat on the cabin. I thought she must faint outright, but she controlled herself.

"Will you get a tourniquet, Mr. Van Weyden," Wolf Larsen called to me.

I hesitated. Her lips moved, and though they formed no words, she commanded me with her eyes, plainly as speech, to go to the help of the unfortunate man. "Please," she managed to whisper, and I could but obey.

By now I had developed such skill at surgery that Wolf Larsen, with a few words of advice, left me to my task with a couple of sailors for assistants. For his task he elected a vengeance on the shark. A heavy swivel-hook, baited with fat salt-pork, was dropped overside; and by the time I had compressed the severed veins and arteries, the sailors were singing and heaving in the offending monster. I did not see it myself, but my assistants, first one and then the other, deserted me for a few moments to run amidships and look at what was going on. The shark, a sixteen-footer, was hoisted up against the main-rigging. Its jaws were pried apart to their greatest extension, and a stout stake, sharpened at both ends, was so inserted that when the pries were removed the spread jaws were fixed upon it. This accomplished, the hook was cut out. The shark dropped back into the sea, helpless, yet with its full strength, doomed to lingering starvation—a living death less meet for it than for the man who devised the punishment.

NEW FROM POPULAR LIBRARY